M000287939

"The Gift of the Wild Things"

The Life of Caroline Dormon

Courtesy Northwestern
State University

"The Gift of the Wild Things":

The Life of Caroline Dormon

by Fran Holman Johnson

Published by
The Center for Louisiana Studies
University of Southwestern Louisiana

Library of Congress Catalog Number: 90-80609
ISBN Number: 0-984940-55-5

The Center for Louisiana Studies
P.O. Box 40831
University of Southwestern Louisiana
Lafayette, LA 70504-0831

For

Ron

"I was born with something—I call it 'the gift of the wild things'—and because I am simple myself, and have a sympathetic heart, I can understand animals and simple people to an unusual degree. I see, too, so much that others miss. When I know so many lovely things, I feel greedy in keeping them all to myself."

Caroline Dormon in application for a Guggenheim Fellowship, 1942.

Contents

Preface

"I think it would be better to omit the word *Introduction* and merely head the chapter *WHY?* When people see the words *Preface* and *Introduction,* they simply flip the pages!"[1] Thus Caroline Dormon writes to John Macrae, publisher of Harper and Row. With apology to Dormon, though, I offer these introductory remarks.

Notwithstanding the processed materials housed at Northwestern State University which are available for researching the life of Caroline Dormon, some materials are sealed and presently unavailable for study. Also, most of the Dormon coterie is now deceased. Such events limited the scope of this work, particularly the early years of Dormon's life.

Secondly, biography is typically presented in pure chronological form. However, Dormon's life does not altogether allow for such conventional representation; therefore, the events of her life are categorically grouped within broad time frames.

Next, Caroline Dormon was a character, yet this first book of her life highlights her major contributions. Everyone who knew Carrie had a "story" to relate about her, but this work is not primarily anecdotal. In addition, this work is introductory, rather than comprehensive. An effort has been made, insofar as is possible, to present the life of Dormon through her own words.

Lastly, I echo Linne's familiar entreaty:

> If you have found errors in me, your superior knowledge must excuse them. Who does not err while perambulating the domain of Nature? Who can observe everything with accuracy?
>
> Correct me as a friend, and I as a friend will respond with kindness.

[1]Caroline Dormon, letter to John Macrae, October 29, 1963, Folder 1016, Caroline Dormon Collection, Cammie G. Henry Research Center, Watson Memorial Library, Northwestern State University, Natchitoches, Louisiana.

Acknowledgments

In a letter to a friend one year before her death, Caroline Dormon wrote:

> Am getting a little writing done, but company exhausts me so that I can't do anything for several days. There is a perfect wave of people wanting to write me up—must think I'm going to die soon! Am giving data to two libraries, and next time someone wants to write a thesis on me, I'll just refer 'em to a library! The last one who came brought THREE women with her—and they got their visit out . . . left me limp![1]

Part of my indebtedness is to Northwestern State University of Louisiana, the repository of the Dormon Papers, a collection which consists of over 120 cubic feet of processed materials. Former archivist Carol Wells, former associate Mildred Lee, and present archivist Mary Linn Bandaries were helpful and kind during my work at NSU.

Richard and Jessie Johnson, the only curators of Briarwood, inexpressibly assisted me, supplying additional documents and relating valuable non-recorded information and even allowing my family and me to live at Briarwood. With vast knowledge of their own and a lifetime friendship with Carrie, Richard and Jessie maintain the flame of life at Briarwood, the Caroline Dormon Nature Preserve.

I owe much to my daughter, Jennifer, who worked with me during the initial part of my research at NSU, and to my husband, Ron, whose Mother's Day gift to me in 1987 was an excursion to Briarwood, an excursion from which this work derives. Jennifer and Ron, as well as my mother and my brother Tom, have all lovingly supported this project.

I wish to extend gratitude to Glenn R. Conrad and the staff of the Center for Louisiana Studies for appreciating the merits of Caroline Dormon and for affirming the significance of this Louisiana life.

Finally, I express my sincere appreciation for the life and the legacy of Caroline Coroneos Dormon. No person can adequately be recorded in words. Carrie cannot be capsulized in epithets such as "Audubon of Wild Flowers," "a female Thoreau," "wood nymph," or "Queen of the Forest Kingdom." Through the most ordinary of things—birds, flowers, trees, people—she lived the most extraordinary life.

[1]Caroline Dormon, typed note, January 30, 1970, on display at Briarwood.

"The Gift of the Wild Things":

The Life of Caroline Dormon

THE PIONEER AND THE PATTERN

> For the first time in my life I have kept a diary a whole year! No, I haven't written in it every day—it would have been inexpressibly dull if I had. Even *I* could never have borne reading it over. But there are longer gaps than I intended. But that is typical of my life.[1]

Although there are gaps in the entries, Caroline Dormon maintained journals and diaries for almost fifty years of her life. Carrie noted that she continued the journal in order to look back "and see if I can find any pattern."[2]

The pattern that emerges is that of a pioneer. Dormon was the first to promote the establishment of a national forest in Louisiana; she was the first female to be employed by the United States Forestry Department; she was appointed by Franklin D. Roosevelt as the only female member of the De Soto Commission; she was at the forefront of preservation and beautification programs, growing and painting and writing about her native wildflowers and wildlife. Her knowledge of plants and birds and Indians came largely from personal observation and study, patterns learned in her early years from her parents. She also read widely and corrresponded extensively with amateurs and professionals who shared her various interests.

Often a letter is dated with an epithet such as "day after the storm," "summer solstice," or "old June—and how I dread the next four months." On letters, Carrie sometimes sketched flowers or birds for ornament. Occasionally the epistles contained instructions like the following: "After digesting this letter, will you be so good as to burn it? If you don't, I shall never pen you another! Nothing makes me blush so much as to see my letters lying in desks at my friends' homes."[3] Sometimes she admonished "Fire, don't file." Or "I have had a miserable cold, so burn this letter to destroy any possible germs."[4] Frequently Carrie's messages contained postscripts reminding correspondents of the correct spelling of *Dormon,* which was often misspelled *Dorman.*

Eventually, Carrie had a telephone installed for communication. At first, though, she had the phone installed at the nearby house of Nora

Patterson, a black woman who worked for her. Carrie explained: "If you want to phone me, call for me at 2742 Saline. (But *not* at night, as phone is not in my house—I would never get any work done with one of these party-line country phones ringing all day long!)"[5]

Carrie's innumerable interests left her little time to socialize, but she delighted visitors with her knowledge and charm. Often visitors left with seeds and plants from Briarwood. Although she once wrote "Put on my tombstone, KILLED BY COMPANY,"[6] she enjoyed discerning visitors and would remonstrate overdue visitors or lapsed correspondents with "Are you dead or drowned?" or "Did you forget me?"[7] Over a life of eighty-three years, Carrie established many close friendships. Her coterie included eminent foresters and botanists as well as Cammie Henry, Lyle Saxon, François Mignon, Ada Jack Carver, and Elizabeth Lawrence.

Cammie Henry, the Gertrude Stein of Melrose, and Carrie shared many interests. They addressed each other as "mate" or "partner," exchanging letters that included newspaper clippings, flower seeds, and samples of their own prose and poetry. It was at Melrose that Carrie met Lyle Saxon. "I had a sassy letter from Lyle, and it did me more good than a tonic,"[8] Carrie wrote her "mate." A journal entry dated July 20, 1937, records a visit from Lyle.

> Lyle came unexpectedly (he wired Miss Cammie, of course) on Friday night. He is in fine spirits over his book, *Children of Strangers,* and well he may be. It is a splendid piece of work. He has done a difficult piece of writing with delicacy, yet strength. Thank goodness he has got this off his chest at last. Now there is no telling *what* he will do, for he is truly gifted. He gave me a copy of his book and was I glad! He wrote in a characteristic autograph.[9]

Lyle encouraged Carrie in her writing. In the waiting room of a New Orleans physician, Lyle had casually found an article written by Carrie: "I read 'Magic Water' and liked every word of it. Now don't be a fool and deprecate. It is a damned good piece of work. There were some magic words in it, along with the water. My hat is off to you Ma'am."[10]

Sketch by Lyle Saxon for Caroline Dormon, 1935.

Courtesy Northwestern State University

TO PO' CARRIE.*
(With a curt nod towards Wordsworth.)

She dwelt among untrodden ways
In far-off Briarwood:
A maid that I am quick to praise
For being very good.

A violet by a mossy stone,
(Half-hidden from po' me)
Sweet as a jay when only one
Is yelling in the tree.

And there beside a rippling brook,
(Like Mary in Her manger!)
She writ herself a flower-book
In praise of the shy-stranger.

All day, all night, she labored so,
Lying amid Hustonia,
The Ace4r-rubrum blushed and said:
"That girl will get pneumonia!"

She dwelt alone, and few did know
When Carrie ceased to stir,
But she is in her grave, and OH!
The difference to *her!*

*Mock poem sent to Dormon by Lyle Saxon.

It was this mutual regard which, perhaps, allowed Carrie to relate to Lyle the following:

> Now, because you have been very, very good, I'll tell you one of the dark secrets of my life. . . . my middle name is Coroneos—named for my g-g-grandmother, a Greek lady. . . . I learned when I was a kid NOT to tell my middle name—the girls would go off in gales of laughter (whatever gales are).[11]

Melrose also connected Carrie with François Mignon. He and Carrie were of the "stay-put persuasion." They visited at Melrose and at Briarwood, and they corresponded. "Here it is almost midnight, and a mighty odd time to be doing correspondence. But your letter came today, and I want to thank you for it before folding up my beard,"[12] François wrote. He addressed Carrie as "Primavera," "Wood's Miss," "Wild Goose," and "Elusive Sprite" and often asked her advice on "horticultural points as well as particulars in human behavior." He, too, praised Carrie's prose: "You covered the canvas so magnificently that not a shading must be altered, not a word or punctuation changed."[13]

At Melrose Ada Jack Carver and Carrie renewed their acquaintance. They were native Louisianians who had attended college in Marion, Alabama, together. They both enjoyed nature outings and flowers and writing. Frequently they exchanged drafts of poems and stories for the other's perusal. It was Ada Jack's son David Snell who memorialized Carrie in the February 1972 issue of *The Smithsonian*. In that article, Snell recounts a visit to Briarwood when he was four or five. Virginia, Carrie's sister, had taken him with her on a trip to Saline to secure a block of ice. On their way home, Virginia crashed into a pine tree.

> Badly shaken but not hurt, we scrambled out to survey the damage. There was a crimp in the fender. The radiator had been caved in and water and steam were gushing out. But what appalled Virginia and the only thing she bent over to inspect was a gaping white wound, the size of a man's hat, on the tree. She made me help her push the car back onto the lane and then some distance along it, until she could nudge the front end against another tree, to

> make it appear that the crash had taken place there. Then, before we walked to the clearing for help, we returned to the injured tree and covered the wound with fallen branches and pine straw—because Virginia was terrified of what her sister Carrie might say.[14]

Carrie established friendships outside the Melrose circle as well. Her friendship with Elizabeth Lawrence began with a mutual respect for work with flowers. This friendship was also professional, for Lawrence asked Carrie to illustrate one of her books. The two exchanged many letters sharing their love of flowers. Carrie penned her North Carolina friend, "Why don't we live near enough for me to phone you 'Come runnin'! This morning is so bright it fairly glistens; magnolias alba superba and denudata waving their white banners, white flowering quinces, masses of snow. . . ."[15]

Locally, Carrie's friends included Mae Nichols of Saline, Thelma Blalock of Saline, Sara Gladney of Baton Rouge, Mr. and Mrs. Ira Nelson of Lafayette, Inez Conger of Arcadia, and Sudie Lawton of Natchitoches. These people and other friends occasionally offered financial help to Carrie, whose means were always meager. Carrie acknowledged these generous gifts: "I long ago decided that [it] *was FALSE* pride not to accept things that FRIENDS want to do. Especially when everyone knows we are po' as a ha'nt! (Wonder what Thoreau and Burroughs used for money? I know Burroughs ate woodchucks, *but he had* to vary that diet a little!)."[16] Friends donated money and materials for the log cabin which stands today at Briarwood. (Carrie, though, personally selected the logs from Briarwood timber.)

Another friend, Mrs. A. F. Storms, bought Carrie a car.

> Now the good news: my dear old friend who is 85 wants to give me a new car!!! My old one has fallen to pieces. . . . You may think I should refuse to let her—but she gets a big kick out of doing for those she loves. . . . Think I will get a Rambler, for owners tell me you really get 28 miles to the gallon. Too, it is a compact, medium-sized car. I want NO FRILLS.[17]

The most significant relationship that Carrie had during her adult life was with her sister, Virginia. Virginia, who was twelve years older, served as the first home demonstration agent in Natchitoches Parish. In all, she was in the educational profession for almost thirty years. Carrie realized the demands of such a life and hoped for personal success so that Virginia could benefit: "I think that I can't bear it if success comes to me too late for her to enjoy it."[18]

When Virginia married George F. Miller in 1921, Carrie accompanied them on their honeymoon. Virginia kept a journal during the odyssey westward, most frequently noting flowers and trees that she and Carrie observed and sights that she and Carrie enjoyed.[19] The marriage did not last, and Virginia filed for and was granted a divorce.[20]

Virginia returned to Briarwood. In addition to her professional work, Virginia did most of the house work and bookkeeping. "Sis made a beautiful pie out of fresh blackberries, so we feasted." Carrie preferred to be outside; however, she often said she "could make pretty good biscuits—but please don't crowd me."[21] Carrie had culinary skill, but her predisposition was elsewhere. In a journal entry from 1937, she recorded: "'The better the day, the better the deed!' I feel a glow of satisfaction. I have just finished making two glasses of jelly and nearly a pint of 'quince honey'—from one huge quince, or quince cydonia. . . ."[22] The journal entry quickly moves from the jelly to the seeds that produced the plant to the joy of flowers to weather to the goodnight whisper of the Brown Thrasher. Carrie wrote nothing else about jelly making.

Virginia also entertained guests when Carrie had to paint or write or garden, and Virginia served as chauffeur for Carrie's flower expeditions and speaking engagements. Although Carrie enjoyed sharing her knowledge and the talks themselves were not difficult, Virginia generally had to coax Carrie into the speaking engagments, for Carrie did not like to leave Briarwood or her work there.

> It certainly is not that I toil over preparing a 'speech.' I always talk absolutely informally, never read a paper, don't even have notes. But I have to 'dress up,' and go away from the things I love. . . . After I have tried to tell them something fresh and sweet right from the woods, there I have to stand, teetering on unaccustomed

> high heels. And, oh, the first wagtail (La. water thrush) may sing that day![23]

Carrie and Virginia supplemented their salaries with occasional lease money as well as other ventures. Both lost teaching jobs during a single mid-term because of the election of Huey Long. (At a speech in Alexandria, Carrie had been heckled by Long supporters.)

Looking for alternative income, the Dormon sisters established a summer camp for girls "in recognition of a very real need for some place where mothers of young girls could send their daughters for a safe, happy, healthful vacation not far from home."[24] According to Carrie, this project had to be abandoned because the girls were eating all of the profits. The sisters also marketed canned vegetables.

Carrie said of Virginia: "Without her I could accomplish little."[25] Virginia offered Carried illimitable loyalty and support. Carrie was, thus, daunted by Virginia's lengthy illness, an illness which resulted from a car accident and which left Virginia invalided and blind. Virginia died in 1954.

Carrie's own health had always been fragile. She queried: "Why did God make me poor and puny?"[26] She frequently suffered from "villainous flu," she broke her hip bone, and she had a "weak heart." Such physical maladies required Carrie to be selective. For example, in 1945, Paul King Rand, Sr., of Alexandria wrote Carrie: "I do not know how much you know of *sub rosa* doings concerning you and what is contemplated but . . . it is planned to approach the State Board of Education and the head of SLU with the hopes of having you appointed to the faculty of that school on a full time basis."[27] Knowing her physical limits, Carrie declined the offer:

> I think you fellows (I know not whom) who have hatched this scheme are swell; if I were a few years younger and 'hitting on all fours,' I could not turn it down. But as it is, I have to 'parcel out' my strength very carefully, working a short while, then resting. Anyone who teaches *well*, gives everything he has. I have taught, and I know.[28]

Despite her guarded health, Caroline Dormon lived eighty-three years, accomplishing many goals and enjoying life: "We oldsters have the best of

Labels placed by the Dormons on canned vegetables.

Courtesy Northwestern State University

Caroline Dormon with "Grandpappy."

Courtesy of John C. Guillet

it. . . . Now we can pause, weigh, re-evaluate, reminisce, and get the best out of it."[29]

In many ways, Caroline Dormon was like the two hundred fifty-year-old longleaf pine she named "Grandpappy." Both Grandpappy and Carrie were beautiful creatures of nature who had survived. When foresters told Carrie that she would outlive Grandpappy, she countered: "I know better—my very soul lives in that beautiful old gnarled and weather-beaten tree. Oh, my the tales he could tell of his rugged survival through the storms of life."[30] Carrie explained the reverence she felt for her companions in nature:

> Am reading Walden once more. But you know, I think John Muir's writing is much finer. His *wildness,* of course, appeals to me. His descriptions are unmatched, I think, in the language. And he, too, is worn out by town and PEOPLE! I can sit right here and watch birds and squirrels. They NEVER overpower me with conversation—and they never ask, 'But don't you get lonely way out here?' I will never get people to believe that I LOVE to be alone! Of course, I'm not really alone—with birds, trees, and flowers—and the different voices of the winds (so different in pines and deciduous trees)—and rain on the shining leaves.[31]

Throughout Carrie's long life, she indefatigably worked to identify and preserve this natural beauty. She worked in many arenas. "I bit off more than I could chew when I was young, and I've been spitting out *ever since*."[32] Yet, Carrie was aware that the apparently ordinary cordiality she shared with nature had something of the extraordinary in it as well:

> I am humbly thankful for my—what? What shall I call it? My secret name is 'the gift of the wild things,' for it includes so much—hearing a bird note above the chatter of a crowd; thrilling at the way twigs gleam against the sky; seeing a thousand things that no one else sees. And the way birds and animals know me is a part of it. One reason for this understanding is—understanding. I never crowd or push myself on them. I never startle them by sudden or violent motions. And I love them. Another part of it is my being able to find a happiness with so little. I am sorry for poor things

who fret and pine for fine clothes and houses and cars. Smug am I? No, just *humbly thankful.*[33]

[1]Caroline Dormon, typed journal entry, January 1, 1938, Cammie G. Henry Research Center, Watson Memorial Library, Northwestern State University, Caroline Dormon Collection, Folder 977. Unless specified otherwise, the citations below refer to this repository and this collection.

[2]*Ibid.*

[3]Caroline Dormon, letter to Mr. Douglas, Folder 101.

[4]Caroline Dormon, letter to Jo Evans, Folder 1403.

[5]Caroline Cormon, letter to Mr. Evans, December 5, 1956, Folder 945.

[6]Caroline Dormon, typed note, April 26, 1969, on display at Briarwood, Saline, Louisiana.

[7]Caroline Dormon, typed note on display at Briarwood.

[8]Caroline Dormon, letter to Cammie Henry, Melrose Scrapbook #213.

[9]Caroline Dormon, typed journal entry, July 20, 1937, Folder 977.

[10]Lyle Saxon, letter to Caroline Dormon, July 22, 1932, Folder 557.

[11]Lyle Saxon, letter to Caroline Dormon, July 22, 1932, Melrose Scrapbook #53.

[12]François Mignon, letter to Caroline Dormon, August 5, 1950, Folder 1464.

[13]François Mignon, letter to Caroline Dormon, December 9, 1950, Folder 1464.

[14]David Snell, *The Smithsonian,* (February, 1972), 32.

[15]Caroline Dormon, letter to Elizabeth Lawrence, February 15, 1959, Elizabeth Lawrence Collection, #26.

[16]Caroline Dormon, journal entry, April 1952, Folder 952.

[17]Caroline Dormon, letter to Elizabeth Lawrence, May (?), 1960, Elizabeth Lawrence Collection, #27.

[18]Caroline Dormon, typed journal entry, June 15, 1937, Folder 977.

[19]Virginia Dormon, typed journal, June 18-August 23, 1921, Folder 1082.

[20]Legal documents recording the divorce of Virginia Dormon, Folder 1312.

[21]Caroline Dormon, typed journal entry, Christmas Day, 1937, Folder 977.

[22]Caroline Dormon, typed journal entry, January 3, 1937, Folder 977.

[23]Caroline Dormon, typed journal entry, January 2, 1937, Folder 977.

[24]Advertisement for Briarwood Camp, Folder 1094.

[25]Caroline Dormon, handwritten note, Folder 1090.

[26]Caroline Dormon, letter to "My very dear friend," on display at Briarwood.

[27]Paul King Rand, Sr., letter to Caroline Dormon, April 26, 1945, Folder 1070.

[28]Caroline Dormon, letter to Paul King Rand, Sr., April 30, 1945, Folder 1070.

[29]Caroline Dormon, typed note, December 2, 1970, on display at Briarwood.

[30]Caroline Dormon, typed note, on display at Briarwood.

[31]Caroline Dormon, letter to Elizabeth Lawrence, Elizabeth Lawrence Collection, #35.

[32]Caroline Dormon, handwritten note, Folder 917.

[33]Caroline Dormon, typed journal entry, May 14, 1937, Folder 977.

THE "DAUGHTY"

Caroline Coroneos Dormon was born on July 19, 1888, at Briarwood, her parents' summer home in Saline, Louisiana. Dormon summarized the focus of her life in a handwritten note:

> Mine is no passing whim—it is a love of a life time. It kept me busy as a child. I often risked neck and limb to see the color of a bird egg, but I came through whole. I knew just when and where to find the first yellow jasmine and where grew the pinkest azaleas. Through adolescence my mind was filled with wholesome, woodsy thoughts, and still I was busy, hearing now the correct names of my birds and wild-flowers and experimenting with little wild gardens.
>
> Since maturity my knowledge of and love for nature have brought to me some of my dearest friends, have been at the heart of my most treasured experiences. . . .
>
> I can slip away to my world of birds and trees and rise serene above them. A swift realization comes that I possess something fine and lovely which no power on earth can take from me.[1]

Caroline Dormon was in many ways an ordinary person. She was the sixth* child born to James Alexander Dormon and Caroline Trotti Sweat Dormon who had married on January 29, 1873, at Briarwood. Comfortable, but not wealthy, the Dormon family particularly valued education and nature.

James Dormon was "a lawyer by profession, a naturalist for love."[2] He attended college at Mt. Lebanon and then worked in the law offices of Judge A. B. George. Virginia, Carrie's only sister, recorded her early reminiscences of their father:

* The Dormons had eight children: James Laurence (1874-1909), a lawyer who married Ruth Marsalis; Virginia Trotti (1876-1954), a teacher and Home Demonstration agent who was briefly married to G. F. Miller; Allen McTyeire (1878-1897); Benjamin Screven (1881-1943), a lawyer who married Nannie Moore; A. B. George (1885-1914), a lawyer; Caroline Coroneos (1888-1971); Edwin Harry (1891-1892); and Paul Gaspar (1895-1901).

Courtesy Northwestern State University

James Alexander Dormon and Caroline Trotti Sweat Dormon.

> My father had pneumonia three times when a young man, which left him rather delicate; but so methodical was he in taking care of himself, that he not only lived past three score, but did a great amount of work. He controlled his habits and appetites more than any other person I have ever known. His devotion to my mother was something you sometimes read about, but seldom see. He usually rose before any of the rest of us, and took a walk about the place. When mother came to the breakfast table, there would be a rose bud, a bunch of violets, or some other dainty flower on her plate. In her last illness, which lasted several months, he abandoned his office, and devoted his entire time to her. He was a wonderful nurse, and when any of us were sick, just to have him lay his hand on our heads and speak in his cheery manner made us feel better immediately. He was the most cheerful person in the world, and no matter how deep were his bitter disappointments and sorrows (and there were many), he turned a smiling face to the world, and never bothered others with his troubles, not even his own children.[3]

Mr. Dormon was esteemed as a lawyer, but he did not become wealthy because he found it difficult to "press" his clients for payments. Although money was never abundant in the Dormon household, the Dormon children were lovingly provided with many opportunities for education—education from reading and from nature.

Learning at his feet, Caroline characterized her father as possessing "magic." He called her "Daughty," and it is clear that she was her father's favorite.[4] He took her with him everywhere: to the Pentecost Place to view the delicious blooms of wild crabapple; to Slide Cut (a mysteriously sunken place on the railroad); to court in Minden and in Homer.

"Daughty, if it's a pretty day Saturday, let's go to Cobb's Pond and see if the perch are biting,"[5] was an invitation from her father that "electrified" her. Cobb's Pond was not only a haven for animals but also for wild flowers. She found Jack-in-the-pulpits that were "a yard tall." The pond was five miles from town; Mama packed lunch for them, and they rode out, Caroline riding behind her father on their large Kentucky mare. Mr. Dormon pointed out the "otter slides," teaching Caroline that animals were ingenious enough to invent amusements for themselves. Carrie recorded this experience:

> Once when I was a little girl, my father took me fishing. 'Come here, daughter' he called; 'I want to show you something worth remembering.'
>
> We were on a high bank, where a curve in the bayou had carved out a wide deep pool. 'There,' he said, pointing, 'is an otter slide.' . . .He told me how these beautiful creatures are so gay and full of fun that they actually invented a game to amuse themselves! The parents and a bunch of pups scoot down this 'slick,' into the water with a joyful splash, under and out—then around again till tired.[6]

On these fishing trips, the Dormons caught plenty of red perch; however, Caroline was more interested in exploring the flora, the wild wisteria and red honeysuckle, that extended out over the pond. She was only five when her father showed her the cunning brown papaw flowers. Papa taught Caroline the names and habits of animals, flowers, and trees. When Papa did not know the name of a species, he would say, "We will have to look this one up."[7] This pattern of research was adopted by Caroline.

In addition to teaching Caroline about nature, Mr. Dormon instilled another interest: the children of nature, the Indians and their culture. Mr. Dormon obtained available bulletins and tracts about Indians and their culture. Caroline listened to her father read from these works before she could read, and she knew by picture many of the Indian chiefs.

Natural things were more valued in the Dormon household than manufactured ones. Mrs. Dormon frequently lamented that she could not wear feathers or fur like the animals, for she did not enjoy shopping for clothes. Virginia, Caroline's twelve year older sister, shopped for her mother since they were the same size. Caroline suspected Virginia of purchasing items she preferred so that she could then "borrow" them. Caroline admired her mother's good sense and vivid personality.[8]

Mrs. Dormon was a bright woman who received formal schooling at a junior college at Sparta, Louisiana. She read voraciously and continued to study throughout her life. At the age of forty-five she took a correspondence course in French. She also served as critic to one of the first literary clubs in North Louisiana, the Young Matron's Club. She wrote stories and poems. She authored *Under the Magnolias*,* a novel that reflects much of

* The novel lists the author's name as Dorman. In a copy of the novel, Carrie penned this note: "There was a controversy over the spelling of the name. My mother favored *an* but my father insisted that the oldest form was *on*."[9]

Virginia Dormon

Courtesy Northwestern State University

what the Dormon household held in esteem: family, education, and nature. Each chapter begins with an epigraph from writers such as Sir Walter Scott and William Shakespeare.[10]

In the novel, several children in the Melton family died in infancy. The Dormon family had lived in this "house of sorrows" as well. When brother Edwin died of whooping cough, Caroline was only four years old. Mrs. Dormon asked Caroline not to sing "Go Tell Aunt Patsy" and "See the Boat Go Round the Bend," songs Caroline sang as she rocked her dolls. The young girl understood that such songs made her mother sad. Caroline's brother James also died as a child. Caroline saved the poem her mother wrote about his death.[11]

In Memoriam

To me a lovely boy was given,
To make more bright my earthly lot,
He made my home a bit of heaven,
Of all the world the sweetest spot,
My heart was full of love and joy,
For little James—my angel boy.

I felt my cup of bliss was full,
As in my arms I clasped my child;
No duty done for him seemed dull,
If but on me my infant smiled,
E'er brighter sunlight filled the place
And flowers bloomed with rarer grace.

I brought our lovely flowers to bloom,
In father's home with sisters dear;
And little thought we of the gloom,
For fell disease now claimed our boy,
And hushed in deep dispair [*sic*] our joy.

Me thinks an angel's smiling face,
Was lingering near with tenderest kiss;
To lure him to that heavenly place,
Where all is love, where all is bliss,
But oh! my world is starless night,
No hope is left, no love, no light.

Oh husband! back to thee I turn,
Back to the home I left so fair;
For that sweet spot I sorely yearn,
For seems our baby must be there.
You kissed our boy. How strange that this,
Should be your last, fond loving kiss.

Oh, Savior, in that home so bright,
Pray Thee, keep my jewel fair;
Until I reach that land of light,
And we are all united there.
Oh blissful thought, divinest joy!
To clasp again my darling boy.

MRS. C. T. DORMON

Arcadia, La.

Another similarity between the fictional Meltons and the Dormons was the value both families placed on education. The Melton's daughter whose education is jeopardized by financial difficulties is called "dear girlie," an address used by Papa Dormon in letters to Caroline when she was at college.[12] The Melton family corresponds with folk in "Brierwood, Louisiany," and eventually moves to the state. Many conversations in the book evidence Mrs. Dormon's knowledge of flora. The conversation between the two major characters, Evelyn Melton and Dr. Laurie Montgomery, provides an example.

> 'Doctor Montgomery, will you tell me what kind of vine this is, twined so beautiful about this oak?'
> 'That is one of our more fragrant and early blooming vines, flowering generally in March, but often in February. The flowers are trumpet-shaped and of a lovely golden hue. It is the yellow jessamine, or, as the botanists call it, *Gelsemiinum sempervirens*.[13]

Almost every paragraph of *Under the Magnolias* includes word pictures of "banks of brilliant chrysanthemums," or "golden arborvitae," or "thick hedges of casino and cherokee" and sounds of birds whose songs made "all stop involuntarily to listen to the exquisite songster, as he gave utterance to his ever changing notes, from triumphant songs to the low, soft cadences, that filled the soul with melancholy."[14] The Meltons (and the Dormons) observed and listened and learned the music and the art nature had to teach.

The novel of Mrs. Dormon recounts folklore of the region. For example, to eat "a half ripe persimmon without making a wry face was proof positive as Holy Writ that the fellow for whom it was named loved you devotedly." Another folk tradition held that bachelors and maidens attending a wedding should carry away a "bit of the bride's cake done up in fancy tissue, to dream on."[15] Although parlors and promenades and provincialities are sentimentally used in the novel, it is a sweet story that underscores the heritage Caroline received.

That heritage had nature at the core. One of Caroline's earliest childhood remembrances is found in her typed notes subtitled "An Autobiography."

> George was the brother next to me, and each of us had a tiny 'garden.' Every spring Mama would give us flower and vegetable seeds to plant but left the planting of them entirely to us. This particular spring, George must have been about six years old, so that would make me three. Evidently my 'green thumb' had not developed, for very few of my seeds even came up. George's not only came up, they grew. I stood my disappointment very well—until Thunbergialata bloomed! It was a tiny vine, but those bright yellow flowers with black centers fascinated me. They undermined my character, for one day I slipped out and dug up one of George's little vines and planted it in my garden! Of course it died, and to this day I can feel the awful weight of guilt. I confessed and cried, but tears did not mend matters.[16]

Mrs. Dormon, though, knew that Caroline had a gift of the "wild things." She turned her own garden in Arcadia over to her daughter. The red clay soil full of iron was especially suited for roses, and the garden was full of old fragrant Damasks. Mrs. Dormon, a brunette, particularly loved yellow and had added to the garden Marchal Neil, placing it on a little frame that soon was dwarfed by the huge golden buds. Caroline inherited a love for and knowledge of those formal flowers, but she also inherited native plants like ferns, violets, and phloxes.

Knowing and appreciating nature were early lessons for the Dormon children. Caroline accompanied her father and brothers on their hunting trips, especially on bird hunts. She did not shoot the animals, but she did use her "sharp eyes" to find the game they shot. The hunters always carried salt and matches in order to prepare dinner in the woods. The hunters dressed the birds, skewered them on a stick, and roasted them over the coals. Occasionally they added yams to the meal, digging remaining sweet potatoes from harvested fields. While the yams roasted in the coals, they continued hunting.

In addition to hunting birds to eat, each spring the Dormon children suffered from "bird nest fever." Ben, the brother next to Caroline, was known to have had the most wonderful bird-egg collection. The children, who had heard that if a human touched the nest the bird would not return, lifted the eggs with a teaspoon. After securing the eggs, Ben blew the eggs hollow, mounted them on cards, and provided identification. Although their father knew scientific names for the birds and the family had an excellent library, Ben used the names the children gave to the birds: "*topknot*," "*tomtit*," "*bullbat*."

Securing the eggs required ingenious equipment and unusual climbing ability. To reach nests, such as Oriole nests, which were at the end of long limbs, the children constructed rope swings . Caroline was held in high esteem by her brothers because of her climbing ability. One day while wandering in the woods, she spied long clear tags of gum exuding from a sweetgum which had been ringed by woodpeckers. The tags—at the right stage—were savory, a natural "bubble gum." (In fact, the children would take the seeds in the black berry of Similax and chew the rubbery covering of the tiny skins into the sweetgum. This concoction produced an especially loud pop, a pop that if made in school generally resulted in the popper standing in the corner.) As Caroline gathered the gum and enjoyed the delight, she noticed birds fluttering about. Near the end of an old and brittle limb, there was a lichen-covered cup. She recognized the birds; they were blue-grey gnatcatchers, a kind Ben did not have. She also knew that the limb would not support Ben's weight. Inching her way to the end of the limb, she found five tiny light-blue eggs. She had no spoon, but she reached and retrieved one egg. She placed the egg in her mouth and carefully climbed down. Victoriously, she ran all the way home. Notwithstanding the spoils she had to show, the boys insisted she take them back to the tree for verification. Although a frail child, Caroline "kept up with the boys."

Bird-nesting required bird-watching. It took keen sight and patience to discover the nests. The Dormon children spent hours behind logs and bushes waiting to see the destination of a bird carrying materials to build a nest. This pleasure lasted until well into summer when the heat diminished their eagerness and they replaced bird-nesting with cooler endeavors such as damming up streams and treehouse building.

The Dormon children were allowed to build a treehouse in the oak in front of their house in Arcadia. The limbs of the tree branched over the street. The children used a rope ladder to enter and simply drew the ladder up to exclude uninvited visitors. They added a crude clay oven on which they could cook. Townspeople drove beneath their tree house, watching curiously the activities. These Dormon children were labeled "wild," especially Caroline whose childhood nickname was "Bad." Caroline had been known to fake falls from trees to make Aunt Fannie scream. Once a neighbor saw Caroline walking on top of the house; he remarked, "That child is as wild as the wind."

Sunday afternoons were frequently spent on walks to nearby Glover's Branch, the Dormon children hunting for wildflowers and wild grapes. This was the "school" they most enjoyed. And nothing was more glorious to the children than being told that they were going "down the country," an epithet for Briarwood. Caroline labeled two milestones in the Dormon household: going to Briarwood and Christmastime. For six months the children looked forward to Christmas; immediately after Christmas they began planning to go "down the country." Six weeks each summer Papa Dormon turned his law practice over to his partner, and the family journeyed to Briarwood. There were no stores along the path, so a wagon of supplies, groceries, and bedding was sent to Briarwood. The Dormon boys were allowed to accompany this supply wagon; they camped out overnight. Caroline was always envious of their privilege. Then very early the next morning, Mr. and Mrs. Dormon, Caroline, and the baby brother left in the surrey with a stout livery team. Virginia, known in the family as "Sis," did not always go to Briarwood with the family, for she was twelve years older than Caroline and frequently remained in Arcadia with cousins to attend parties and socials.

On the way to Briarwood, Caroline began looking for long leaf pines, her most beloved trees. The trees at that time had not been cut; they majestically crowned the sand hills near Briarwood. Their branches allowed enough sunlight through to make visible the carpet of Goats Rue and pink and cream pea flowers. Stopping along the way for the horses to drink, the family watched masses of butterflies on the wildflower carpet. This was the legacy of Caroline Dormon: a family that valued the simple, but beautiful, joys of nature.

Another birthright accorded the Dormon children was an education. Mr. and Mrs. Dormon considered education a priority for their children; all of them were sent to institutions of higher learning. Caroline was sent to The Judson, a private college founded in 1839. She did not want to go away to college but was told that she "had the family reputation to uphold." While at Judson, that family supported her with correspondence.

Caroline entered Judson College, Marion, Alabama, when she was only sixteen, a "tomboy" at an old-fashioned school for young women.

> My first year at college was unhappy. At home, my family [and] so my place was established. I had no idea how to meet strangers and make a place for myself. Then the second year, the girls suddenly decided that I was witty! They would go into gales of laughter at my drolleries. A small thing—but it restored me! I did not have to be pretty, I did not have to have beautiful clothes! I could just be myself.

At Judson, girls were not allowed off campus without a teacher. Caroline, however, was soon excepted from this rule, frequently being sent on errands or permitted to go on nature walks in the woods. No matter where she would be in her life she would always find "escapes." On walks to nearby Gray's Hollow, she discovered many new species such as *Iris eristila, Iris verna*, yellow violets, hepatica, and bloodroot. This love for and knowledge of wild things endeared her to her teachers as well as to her peers. On a walk with her science teacher, Caroline heard a bird's song and remarked, "Isn't that wren sweet?" The teacher asked her where the wren was since she had not seen it. When Caroline explained that she had not seen it, but rather had recognized it by its song, the teacher asked to be taught. Caroline had that rare gift of the wild, and others were already beginning to recognize her talents.

Caroline and thirty classmates graduated in 1907; her degree was in Fine Arts, with emphasis on literature and art. She furthered studied art in a summer workshop at the Natchitoches Art Colony under the direction of Will Stevens. After graduating from Judson, Caroline first returned to Arcadia where Sister was determined to make her a "lady." This apprenticeship had two negative effects. It gave her less time with nature, and, consequently, less time for Papa. There were no quarrels; they just grew apart. Tragically, her mother died the year she graduated from Judson, and her father died just two years later. Caroline felt great remorse at not having had time to become reacquainted with her father and her mother. Tragedy continued. The family home in Arcadia burned only three months later. In less than three years, Caroline would lose both her parents and her home. She would begin her adult years without Papa or Mama or home, but she did have Sister and the sand hills she loved so much "down the country."

Notes

1. Caroline Dormon, handwritten note, Caroline Dormon collection, Cammie G. Henry Research Center, Watson Memorial Library, Northwestern State University, Folder 814.

2. Caroline Dormon, typed notes titled "The Heart of Wildness," Folder 770.

3. Virginia Dormon, typed manuscript titled "Personal Memoirs of James A. Dormon's Daughter," Folder 1330.

4. Caroline Dormon, typed notes titled "The Heart of Wildness," Folder 770.

5. James A. Dormon, conversation recorded by Caroline Dormon, typed notes titled "The Heart of Wildness," Folder 770.

6. *Ibid.*

7. *Ibid.*

8. Caroline Dormon, typed notes titled "The Heart of Wildness," Folder 770.

9. Caroline Dormon, handwritten note in her personal copy of *Under the Magnolias*, Rare Books, Northwestern State University.

10. Caroline Dormon, typed notes titled "Personal Notes," Folder 1056.

11. Caroline Dormon, typed notes titled "The Heart of Wildness," Folder 770.

12. James Dormon, letter to Caroline when she was at Judson, March 19, 1905, Folder 1056.

13. Caroline Trotti Dorman, *Under The Magnolias*. (New York: The Abbey Press, 1903), page 4.

14. Caroline Trotti Dormon, *Under The Magnolias*, page 117.

15. Caroline Trotti Dormon, *Under The Magnolias*, page 123 and page 239.

16. Caroline Dormon, typed notes titled "The Heart of Wildness," Folder 770. Facts on Caroline Dormon and her family presented in the remainder of this Chapter are drawn from "The Heart of Wildness."

Courtesy Northwestern State University

Caroline Dormon
on one of her "escapes."

"MISS CARRIE," THE TEACHER

Robert G. Patrick, president of The Judson, recommended Carrie by stating that she was "well prepared to do excellent teaching in Art." He stated that she had "made a splendid record"[1] at Judson. As as result of this preparation, in 1908 Bienville Parish issued Caroline a five-year certificate to teach youth in the first grade, and in 1910 that same parish issued her another five-year certificate to teach youth sight singing and drawing.[2]

Her first teaching assignment was for first grade in Bienville Parish. In an article in the August 18, 1977, *Natchitoches Times*, Lacey Bishop Weaver reminisced about "Miss Carrie." Weaver spoke of taking a field trip to Carrie's home to see the flowers bloom and of Carrie's particular talents in song. Weaver also recounted one classroom decoration: a turkey Carrie had drawn on the blackboard. The remarkable feature of the drawing was that the splendor of the turkey had been captured through colored chalk, a novelty for 1908.[3]

The next year Carrie taught singing and drawing in the high school at Lake Arthur, Louisiana. She was described by W. S. Streater, manger of Lake Arthur Office of Calcasieu Trust and Savings, as "being of a pleasing disposition and noble character and popular with all who knew her."[4] Teaching in Lake Arthur, she still found time for outings or "escapes," rowing across the lake in a pirougue or galloping (side-saddle, for ladies did not ride astride in those days) over the hills in a March wind. Caroline knew this was her real self; she labelled the other "veneer."

Maintaining the family tradition, she continued to return to Briarwood in the summer. The teaching did not stop in the summer months; young children and adults who wandered by always received lessons in nature. Virginia returned as well, with alacrity assuming the roles of parent, housekeeper, cook, business manager, and sister.

During 1913 and 1914 Caroline corresponded with a young man named "Jamie." He addressed her as "my dearest Carrie" and wrote of the possibilities of her moving to Anniston, Alabama, and teaching there. He argued that she could make just as much money ($75.00). He told her that since he could not come to "c" her, she would have to come to see him. Although the details of their meeting and relationship are vague, Jamie referred to Ben in some of the letters, a reference perhaps to Carrie's brother Ben. In addressing her, Jamie uses a variety of vocatives, including "sweetheart," "dear," "baby," and "queen." A letter from Jamie dated Friday,

October 24, 1913, evidences that Carrie allowed him no liberties even in writing her.

> I will begin this note by apologizing to you for not asking your permission to correspond with you. I am truly sorry that you were so grossly insulted with me for not doing so. I now ask you, with tears in my eyes and a bleeding heart, to give me the honor, pleasure, and distinction of corresponding with you. I will continue by saying that I know of nothing that could offer me more pleasure than writing to you if you should grant my request.[5]

Jamie also made reference to a previous suitor of Carrie's, the "Oil King."

> I heard very straight that you [Caroline] and the 'Oil King' were to be married at the close of your school. Of course, I don't expect you to admit it, but I am inclined to think that it is true. I noticed you failed to mention his name when you write to me. . . . When you get ready to marry him I want you to let me know in time to quit writing and forget that I ever *loved you*. This is the only request I have to make of you.[6]

He does, though, seem to make other requests, including that she be more timely in answering his letters: "I want to hear from you once every week at least, and if you love me half as much as I love you, you will grant my request." He admonished her to ask "the Lord to forgive you for breaking your 'bet.'"[7] Although there are no facts about the end of their relationship, it is plausible that Caroline was not accustomed to reins from anyone. Her first love was and would continue to be "the wild things."

Caroline's brother Ben had also been unsuccessful in persuading Caroline to move to Anniston. Ben had moved to Alabama after serving for several years in Washington as a secretary to Senator Murphy Foster from Louisiana. When Ben began his practice of law in Anniston, he asked Carrie to move in with his family and teach his son Benjamin and several other neighborhood children. In addition to the "nominal fee" from the neighborhood children, Ben offered her room and board:

> . . .Your board and living would cost you nothing and you ought to have enough clothes to pull through on without investing very

> heavily in the wool and leather markets. If you haven't, I can lend you an Army blanket to piece out with.
>
> I don't intend to compete with Dickens or Washington Irving when it comes to holding out gastronomic inducements, but in passing would mildly suggest that we have the following pabulum in stock or in view, viz: Plenty of 'black-eyed' peas; maiz or Indian corn in profusion; peanuts; pop corn; sweet potatoes until the Devil wouldn't have them; Irish potatoes; turnips and greens; collards; onions and canned truck; eggs by the million; frying size chickens and broilers 'til it makes you mad to look at them, and more to hatch this week and next; plenty of milk and butter from our own Jersey cow; home cured hams and bacon and smoked, stuffed sausage (for we have a 175 pound hog in the pen now, fat enough to kill, and will start another pig to fattening shortly.)[8]

These inducements notwithstanding, Caroline chose to remain in Louisiana. By 1917,* she and Virginia had moved to Briarwood and built a small cabin from Briarwood timber.

Because of poor health, Caroline petitioned the superintendent to assign her to a school system in the pine woods rather than in a lake district. Hudson, the superintendent, assigned her to Kisatchie. Boarding with a family in Provencal, Carrie made the twenty-mile trip to Kisatchie School in a wagon pulled by a pair of stout mules. Caroline noticed more than the dirt roads: "Over the rolling hills we wound, through mile after mile of majestic longleaf pines. I was in heaven."[9]

At that time few persons had explored the Kisatchie area. Kisatchie was still a legend. The name had been derived from a tribe of Kichai Indians of the Caddoan stock. They called themselves "Kitsachies." Remains of their pottery and implements such as arrowheads were found near streams and in plowed fields. Caroline joined the small number of folk, mostly hunters from Natchitoches, who had seen the hundreds of square miles of wild rocky hills. The panorama moved Caroline first to dream, then to action.

> The high hills may be seen across Cane River from Derry and

* Although various documents suggest 1918, 1920, and 1922 as dates for permanent Dormon residency at Briarwood, the date used here derives from a handwritten note by Dormon: "In 1917 Misses Virginia and Caroline Dormon built a home and came to live permanently in the community."

> Chopin, and they extend to within a few miles of Sabine River on the west. From Anacoco on the south, they reach to Provencal on the north. The outcrop of Grand Gulf Sandstone—an unusual sight in Louisiana—creates sheer stony bluffs, and small waterfalls in the clear streams. Because of the heavy forests, on the oldest maps it is designated as The Kisatchie Wold. . . . Immediately I began exploring this fascinating region—in a wagon, on horseback, on foot—later in a Ford car. I saw Kisatchie, Little Kisatchie, Sandy, Rocky Creek, Odom's Falls, and the tumbling waters of L'ivrogue. The Great pines come right to the water's edge on these lovely clear creeks, with only an occasional magnolia, and masses of ferns and wild azalea. There the idea was born—all this beauty *must* be preserved for future generations to enjoy.[10]

In 1919 Caroline wrote to the Louisiana Department of Conservation to inquire about the Southern Forestry Congress to be held in New Orleans from January 28 to 30, 1920, and to plant the seeds for her campaign to protect primeval tracts of timber. M. L. Alexander, commissioner of the Department of Conservation, replied, thanking her for her interest, encouraging her efforts to marshall support from the Federation of Women's Clubs, and forwarding to her bulletins about various forestry concerns.[11]

In January at her own expense, Caroline attended the Southern Forestry Congress. The meeting afforded the opportunity to learn what measures were being taken to preserve the forests of southern pines. She had seen the "kingly longleaf pines" mowed down by loggers, and she had seen the inevitable fires which followed. She visited with people who shared her interest in preserving natural forest lands and promoting conservation. Before going to New Orleans, Caroline had written to Mrs. A. F. Storm, president of the Louisiana Federation of Women's Clubs, to arrange a conference with her. In their meeting, Caroline shared with Mrs. Storm her dream of saving a virgin tract of timber. Mrs. Storm, a naturalist herself, pledged "whole-hearted" support and invited Caroline to head the Forestry Division of the Louisiana Federation of Women's Clubs. She also appointed Carrie as one of the state's seven delegates to the Fifteenth Biennial Convention of the General Federation of Women's Clubs in Des Moines, Iowa, in June 1920.[12]

In addition to meeting Mrs. Storm at the Southern Forestry Congress, Caroline also met with Henry Hardtner, known as the father of reforestation in the South, and Col. Henry S. Graves, chief forester of the United States.

Both men listened to Caroline talk of Kisatchie, of her hope to preserve a primeval forest. They shared Caroline's enthusiasm, but the work ahead would depend on the perseverance of this fragile dynamo. A note in Caroline's own script suggests her motivation: "I am not doing this in execution of a duty thrust upon me, but voluntarily, joyously, for the pure love of it."[13] In this same handwritten note, she outlined her plan of attack. First, she would publicize the forest idea through newspaper articles. Next, there would be an appeal for money to purchase the tracts of virgin timber as well as cutover timber to be used for agricultural and scientific experimentation and education. The order of appeal would be lumbermen, oil men, chambers of commerce, Federation clubs, and legislature.

Caroline's deep interest in forestry was noticed. In March of 1920 R. D. Forbes,* then secretary-treasurer of the Louisiana Forestry Association, wrote Dormon to inform her that President Hardtner had appointed her to the Legislative Committee of the Louisiana Forestry Association. The committee's task would be "to map out a plan of work and submit such recommendations to the legislature."[14] Immediately the Department of Forestry and its auxiliaries began requesting Miss Dormon's help with various projects. She was asked to devise outlines for programs of forestry education and to revise a school text on forestry. When in August of 1920, R. D. Forbes, the superintendent of Forestry, wrote to thank Dormon for her revision, he told her that a teacher's committee would be formed "to pass upon the entire conservation text"[15] and that she would be appointed to the committee.

Caroline and her sister Virginia continued to explore the Kisatchie area, always inviting interested parties like Mrs. Storm and Mr. Forbes to view the untouched forests. She studied available maps and plotted her own. She investigated the ownership of the areas and determined which lumber companies owned the most desirable tracts. Using her title as chairman of forestry for the Louisiana Federation of Women's Clubs, Caroline contacted these companies in the following manner:

> Dear Sir:
>
> Have you ever traveled through a real forest of longleaf pines? Your syndicate owns a great area in the sand-hills of North Louisiana, as lovely a stretch of country as one can find. If you

* Forbes was a graduate of the Yale School of Forestry who often suggested "It is better to raise trees than taxes."

> have ever seen it, I feel sure the beauty of it must have gripped you . . . . Our plan is for a park of a thousand acres, at least six hundred and forty of which shall be primeval longleaf pine forest. We want it located where at least one stream will flow through, with its accompanying growth of beech and magnolia. Will you sell to the Federation such a piece of timbered land at an average of $100.00 per acre? Of course, we realize this would be a great concession on your part; but this is in no way [a] business proposition. We are appealing to you for the sake of all that is beautiful and uplifting in a rather sordid world, to do this thing for the people of the state in which you have vast holdings.
>
> What more splendid monument could you leave to do honor to your name? And let me say this: We will find some very sure and beautiful way of telling the world that it was through your generosity that we were enabled to purchase this beautiful park. . . .[16]

Caroline sent a copy of this letter to Mrs. Storm, asking for her suggestions and criticism. Mrs. Storm returned the copy with a handwritten note across the top: "Not a [single] criticism. It is OK—should melt his heart."[17] Caroline continued her campaign of correspondence, melting hearts and minds. She wrote J. B. White, head of the syndicate which owned the Four L and three other tremendous mills in North Louisiana. He replied, promising support and offering assistance.[18]

Although support was growing, Caroline met opposition and refusal. One official in the J. A. Bentley Lumber Company, of Zimmerman, Louisiana, argued that the longleaf pines presently mature in Louisiana needed to be harvested. Refusing to dispose of any of his timberlands for the project, he suggested that Dormon find an area of cutover land and reforest it with trees, an activity he thought would be "interesting work for your club."[19] To another dissenter, P. A. Bloomer, Caroline wrote as Thomas Paine would have written:

> I can see your objections to our plan are entirely reasonable, from your point of view; and I frankly admit that I am asking you to lay aside, for a little while, cold reason and business judgment. . . . I have driven and tramped for miles through these uniquely beautiful forests (belonging to your company) and we are asking you to sell us only *one half* of a *section*.[20]

Undaunted by criticism, Caroline continued her campaign, writing public and elected officials as well as interested citizens. She was simultaneously continuing her work as forestry chairman. She devised a competition for the Boys Reforestation Clubs of Louisiana. The contestants, boys between ten and eighteen, were to plant commercially valuable trees on one acre of ground or scientifically care for three acres of tree seedlings, protecting the growth from fire, disease, insects so that plans could be made for reforestation. The Great Southern Lumber Company of Bogalusa provided five hundred dollars in prizes. This competition publicized the value of planting and protecting trees.[21]

Dormon's efforts to promote forestry awareness and her ability to plan and organize forestry events were not unnoticed. Commissioner M. L. Alexander sent Dormon a letter November 26, 1921, stating that he had been so favorably impressed with her interest and work that he was attempting to make a place for her in the forestry division, probably in education and publicity. He suggested a meeting date of December 5 for himself, Caroline, and V. H. Sonderegger, then superintendent of Forestry. The forestry division was interested enough to pay her expenses to this interview in New Orleans.[22]

Notes

1. Robert G. Patrick, letter of recommendation, June 30, 1910, Caroline Dormon Collection, Cammie G. Henry Research Center, Watson Memorial Library, Northwestern State University, Folder 1096.

2. Teaching Certificates of Caroline Dormon, Folder 1096.

3. Lacey Bishop Weaver, Natchtoches Times, August 18, 1977.

4. W. S. Streater, letter of recommendation, July 6, 1910, Folder 1096.

5. Jamie, letter to Caroline Dormon, October 24, 1913, Folder 1070.

6. *Ibid.*

7. Jamie, letter to Caroline Dormon, undated, Folder 1070.

8. B. S. Dormon, letter to Caroline Dormon, August 6, 1921, Folder 1042.

9. Caroline Dormon, typed notes, "The Story of Kisatchie," Folder 1092.

10. *Ibid.*

11. *Ibid.*

12. *Ibid.*

13. Caroline Dormon, handwritten notes, Folder 368.

14. Henry E. Hardtner, President of Louisiana Forestry Association, quoted by R. D. Forbes, letter to Caroline Dormon, March 19, 1920, Folder 393.

15. R. D. Forbes, letter to Caroline Dormon, August 1920, Folder 393.

16. Caroline Dormon, letter to Mr. O. W. Fisher, Seattle, Washington, December 14, 1920, Folder 658.

17. Mrs. A. F. Storm, handwritten note on Dormon's letter to Mr. O. W. Fisher, Seattle, Washington, December 14, 1920, Folder 658.

18. J. B. White, Kansas City, Missouri, letter to Caroline Dormon, Folder 658.

19. J. A. Bentley Company, initialed EWZ (E. W. Zimmermann), letter to Caroline Dormon, February 3, 1921, Folder 659.

20. P. A. Bloomer, letter to Caroline Dormon, June 9, 1921, Folder 365.

21. Caroline Dormon, typed rules for Boys Reforestoration Clubs Contest, Folder 377.

22. M. L. Alexander, letter to Caroline Dormon, November 26, 1921, Folder 360.

A VOICE CRYING FOR THE WILDERNESS

Dormon's employment was noteworthy. She was the first women to be hired in the Louisiana forestry division.* Because there was no job description for her position, M. L. Alexander and V. H. Sonderegger allowed her to plan her work. She created Louisiana's first program of conservation education. She petitioned the state superintendent of schools for his cooperation. In December of 1921, she began visiting schools, making talks and illustrating them with photographs and slides, and even planting trees on school grounds. The superintendent of education sent circulars to parish superintendents and school principals, asking that they implement Dormon's suggestions. Dormon sent out lists of reference books, bulletins, and other literature to the school libraries. She wrote school principals, offering to supply materials and lecturers (most often herself) for their schools. She asked each principal to complete a questionnaire so that she would know what had been done to promote forestry education and what still needed to be done.[1]

She asked seven questions:

1. Has forestry been taught in any grade or department this school year?
2. How many forestry bulletins have you on hand? Wild life bulletins?
3. Have you had slides on forestry subjects to show to you students?
4. Have you a stereoptican for showing slides?
5. Did the school as a whole or any of the grades observe Arbor Day?
6. How many trees have been planted on the school grounds this year?
7. How many trees have the pupils planted at their homes or other places?[2]

Even in the questionnaire two concerns are apparent: educating the public, especially children, about forestry and promoting the planting of trees.

She was deluged with invitations to speak to local and state groups. P. H. Griffith, president of the Louisiana Teacher's Association, invited her to address elementary and rural teachers at their state meeting.[3] She knew the necessity of teaching the teachers. Their interest would be the example for

* It is commonly held that Dormon was the first female hired in forestry in the entire United States.

their pupils. The invitations also came from outside the state. Roy L. Hogue, president of the Southern Forestry Congress, extended the following request to Caroline to speak to the congress in Jackson, Mississippi, in 1922.

> I am sure that we are all delighted to see, through the columns of the trade journals, that you are devoting your time to spreading the forestry doctrine in the Louisiana schools. . . . We want you to follow [the address by the Mississippi State Superintendent of Education] with 1500 or 2000 words from the point of view of one who is actually teaching the children foresty.[4]

At the Mississippi congress, she met Col. W. B. Greeley, chief forester. Caroline described him as a reserved man who "promised nothing" but took "copious notes." At the end of their long conversation, Greeley explained that Louisiana did not have an enabling act and, consequently, that no national forest could be purchased in the state. Caroline now understood why Chief Graves had not proceeded with the project even though he had listened so enthusiastically at the Southern Forestry Congress in New Orleans. Caroline's reply to Col. Greeley was typical: "We will fix that."[5]

Although Caroline's singular dream was to preserve the ancient forests of Louisiana, her work schedule was diverse and full. Bonnell H. Stone, chairman of the Georgia Forestry Committee of the Southern Forestry Congress, heard her talk in Jackson and invited her to speak at the Georgia Forestry Convention to be held a few months later in June of 1922.[6] It is clear that she was making an impact in the forestry world, and it is equally clear that she was charting a new course in her forestry work. M. L. Alexander, commissioner of the Department of Conservation, approved an increase in her salary to $100.00 a month because of the good work she had done for the department.[7] Her immediate superior, Superintendent of Forestry V. H. Sonderegger, wrote her in September, 1922.

> I wish you would write me a general summary report of your activities from the day you started work for the department, giving the ideals and purposes you have in view, the plans and methods you use to distribute these ideas, and also the plans and methods you use to establish forestry in the minds of different classes of children. What I want is a general history of your work as I am writing a story of the reforestation movement, and inasmuch as the

> schools are now on the verge of recognizing it, I want to bring our system to the front and use your work as a special example of what can be done outside of educational institutions.[8]

Although Sonderegger referred to the work as "our system," he did not seem to know the "ideals," "purposes," "plans," "methods," or "general history" of the system. Further, *her* "general summary report" will be used as a basis for his story. Superintendent Sonderegger became increasingly more demanding of Dormon:

> To date I have received no information or description whatsoever of your blue print process although I am hearing from everybody else that you are attempting something of this sort. As stated previously, I think it advisable to confer with me before attempting to do anything at the expense of the department or the time of the department.[9]

Carrie answered:

> The blue print process is no innovation of mine; it is quite old, I understand, and very simple. With regard to the letter I wrote Major Lee at camp about the blue-prints; last summer when I visited the camp, I saw his dendrology students drawing the leaves, and they did not get the veining very well. After I had tried out the prints this summer, I thought I would tell Major Lee of it, as the method would be fine for his classes. It never occurred to me that you would care to be troubled about so trivial a matter. . . . As to my using the time of the Department, very little of it has been used for my blue-print work, as I have tested out the method on Sundays, and during my vacation. Also, in this regard, I think I can say without boasting that the Department has received full value for what has been paid me.[10]

Sonderegger further admonished her: "It is a very embarrassing policy for you to be travelling throughout the State and not paying hotel bills by staying with friends."[11] Carrie had stayed with friends who would not allow her to pay. Her friends had insisted that she not pay, and the state had been saved hundreds of dollars. Sonderegger also questioned the amount of time she spent working on reports and studying. He capsulized his disapproval with: "My criticism. . . is the manner of [your] doing the work and not informing me of its nature. As I previously told you, all the work of the forestry division is subject to my approval and I have objected to your discussing the various phases of work with others and not with me direct."[12]

Such conflicts increased. With regret, Caroline resigned. In a letter to Dudley Berwick, commission of conservation, she wrote:

> It is impossible for me to continue under Mr. Sonderegger and retain my dignity and self-respect. Therefore, this is to offer my resignation, to take effect September first [1923]. If you care to have explanations, I shall be glad to give them.
>
> My love for the work is proved, it seems to me, by the fact that I worked for forestry two years at my own expense, before I was employed by the Department.
>
> My interest in conservation has in no degree lessened; and, as Chairman of Conservation in the Federation of Women's Clubs, and as an individual, I shall gladly cooperate with you at any time in the great work which you represent.[13]

Berwick accepted her resignation because Caroline had stated that "no arrangement could be made whereby [she] could continue to work under Mr. Sonderegger"[14] and because the department had no other positions available. Berwick did ask that Caroline arrange to see him at her "first opportunity" so that they could discuss plans to enable her to continue her good work under his supervision.

Caroline had severed her official connection, but she did as she had said she would do: she continued working through the Federation of Women's Clubs and as an individual for forestry conservation. By this time, R. D. Forbes was able to secure a copy of Florida's enabling act. Now Caroline needed someone to draft similar legislation for Louisiana. Caroline had a resource person she knew to be partial to her causes, her brother Ben. Ben, who still called Caroline by her childhoood nickname "Bad," was an attorney in Anniston, Alabama. She knew that Ben would help with the forestry legislation. The bill Ben drafted for the Louisiana Legislature had three main sections. First, the draft would give the federal government the consent of Louisiana to acquire by purchase, gift, or condemnation lands necessary for the establishment of national forests in the state. Second, power would be extended to the federal government so that it could make rules and regulations for the administration, control, and protection of the lands acquired. Third, previous laws which limited purchases of lands in Louisiana would be repealed.[15]

After the enabling bill had been drafted, Caroline directed her efforts to publicizing the bill in order to gain support for its passage. She argued that the lands would be primarily non-agricultural properties, that much of the land to be acquired was deteriorating from erosion, that the lands could be put to work growing trees, and that the lands could by used by the public. To those who opposed the land purchases by the federal government because the lands would be tax exempt, Dormon countered that Louisiana would receive thirty-five per cent of all gross receipts from the forest.[16] Then she sent State Senator Henry Hardtner a copy of the proposed act. He replied: "This is a good measure, and I will include it in my omnibus forestry bill."[17] He handled the proposal in the senate, and a Mr. Alexander introduced it in the house. The bill was approved.[18]

In addition to this legislative concern, Dormon was continuing to garner support for a forest. She wrote the Committee on Preservation of Natural Conditions of the Ecological Society of America. V. E. Shelford, head of Research and Publication, responded, characterizing Kisatchie Wold as "a place of exceptional value from various points of view. The presences of a large amount of game and the diversity of plant life make it a rare situation for this part of the United States."[19] Dormon was grateful for such encouragement, but she knew much was left to be accomplished.

Next, Col. Greeley sent W. W. Ashe to visit with Dormon. Ashe was the officer in the United States Forest Service who had determined land purchases in the eastern parts of the United States. Caroline and her sister escorted Ashe all over Kisatchie, showing him the virgin longleaf pine forest and the cutover lands that were in need of reforestation. He made many trips to observe and evaluate the area. He was convinced. By early 1925 he wrote to Dormon: "You will be pleased to know that one of these tentative purchase units embraced the Kisatchie Hills about which you write. . . . It is believed that Louisiana will be one of the first states within the southern pine belt which will receive the benefits of . . . extension."[20] Ashe continued to keep Dormon informed about the progress from Washington. Sending her a copy of the news release announcing the authority to purchase land in Louisiana, he added a handwritten note that credited Dormon for the success of this project: "Congratulations, Miss Dormon."[21]

Although state and federal legislation was now in place to make possible the purchase of lands, the national forest was not yet a reality.

Caroline presented the plan to Congressman James B. Aswell, Sr., who agreed to do anything he could to help. Dormon, realizing that this project would require funding far beyond her small means, appealed to Judge Whitfield Jack, who was a nature lover and a personal friend of R. T. Moore, E. A. Frost, and other lumbermen who owned land at Kisatchie. The judge pledged his support.[22]

Then, according to Dormon, fate intervened: "The five men in Louisiana who had been most interested in the project died—within the space of two years! And Mrs. Storm, who had enthusiastically supported the undertaking, moved to South Carolina."[23] Ashe, though, returned to Louisiana with news. He told Caroline that the Forest Service was purchasing areas for ecological studies and that her tract of virgin pine would be included in the purchases. Knowing of her enormous efforts, he released this information to Caroline before the public announcement.

Much work remained. Lumber companies had continued swapping properties. Caroline made lists of the various ownerships and began contacting them. In particular, Caroline was interested in Crowell-Spencer Lumber Company, a company that owned the tract of virgin timber Caroline had determined to save. Caroline personally went to see Stamps Crowell in Alexandria. He gave her a written promise to sell the timber at a reasonable figure:

> Any plan tending to perpetuate a portion of our original forest for the entertainment and instruction of the rising and succeeding generations, has certainly my fullest approval and endorsement.
>
> Be assured that my support of your plan shall be at all times fully commensurate with that of any individual citizen having the best interest of 'the greatest good for the greatest numbers' at heart.[24]

He further thanked her for her personal efforts, expressing his wish that she should receive "ample reward" for striving to benefit so many. He also encouraged her to act expeditiously since the company was presently ready to build tram-roads into the area.

By 1927 Caroline had accepted another position with the Louisiana Forestry Division. Her business card boasted two positions: "Supervisor, Forestry Education of the Department of Conservation" and "Chairman of Forestry, Louisiana Federation of Women's Clubs." These positions again relied heavily on Carrie's "teaching" skills. For example, as supervisor of forestry education, she developed such a suitable tree-study program that T. H. Harris, superintendent of Education, accepted the recommendation for the program without requiring her to make a presentation to him in Baton Rouge. Harris asked parish school superintendents to write directly to the Forestry Division of the Department of Conservation to secure copies of the program for use in their schools.[25]

The tree study for schools was divided according to grades. Caroline recommended that students in the first, second, and third grades be introduced to nature songs and poems and stories, "the chief aim [being] to cultivate in the minds of the children a wholesome respect and love for trees." She wanted these young students to be introduced to the reciprocal relationships in nature. "They should be taught that the birds help protect the tree by eating injurious insects, while trees furnish homes and food for the birds."[26] For class activities, she suggested that the children gather leaves from trees on the schoolground, learn the names of these trees, color and draw leaves and trees, and even plant seeds of various trees. The goal of tree study for fourth and fifth graders shifted to protection of trees. This study of preservation would intensify in the sixth and seventh grades. Dormon wanted each adolescent to develop an appreciation for forests, an appreciation that necessarily included conservation. In all grades, field work was encouraged.

R. D. Forbes, who had secured for Caroline a copy of the Florida enabling act, characterized these teaching tactics:

> . . . Miss Dormon visited the schools of the state regularly and instructed the school teachers in the teaching of simple forestry lessons. Her methods were dictated by sound common sense and a profound appreciation, through personal experience, of the crowded condition of modern curricula. She showed the teachers how forestry material could be used to illustrate and enliven the courses of nature study, commercial and physical geography, botany, 'local' studies, and a large number of other courses already being given. She did not ask the teachers to teach forestry in addition to all of their other work, but showed them how it might be woven into existing studies.[27]

Her teaching became a campaign for conservation. She designed a forestry essay contest for Louisiana schools. High school students were asked to address "Why we must stop forest fires in Louisiana." Caroline procured prize money so that the first prize winner would received $50.00; second, $25.00; third, $10.00. Hundreds of students in over seventy schools entered the contest. The prize-winning essay was printed and distributed throughout the state.[28]

To further educate the public about the destructiveness of fire in the woods, Caroline painted a scene-in-action of a forest fire. There were other submissions for the scene-in-action, but the Department of Conservation deemed Caroline's "unquestionably the best."[29] The oil was displayed at the biennial of the General Federation of Women's Clubs, at the Louisiana State Fair in Shreveport, at the Louisiana Federation of Women's Clubs Convention, at the Southern Forestry Congress, and at local fairs. A number of duplicates were made and used throughout the South. In order to extend the concept of forest-fire prevention, Carrie designed a cover for school books. Over a million school book covers were printed and distributed.[30]

Also, Arbor Day booklets were printed and sent to schools and clubs. In the booklet were suggestions for celebrating Arbor Day, including songs, poems, and dedicatory remarks to be used for tree-planting ceremonies. Nursery records show that over 40,000 trees were given to schools and clubs to plant as part of this program. The booklet offered a complete outline of forestry study as a part of geography or civics classes. As part of the Arbor Day celebration, Dormon devised a contest of questions whose answers were names of Louisiana trees. Students were allowed one minute to answer riddles such as the following:

1. A game fish and something the tree produces.
2. Good to chew.
3. To languish, or long for.
4. A small body of water partially surrounded by land.
5. A long green vegetable.
6. Name of a flying machine.
7. Left when wood burns.
8. Not the younger.
9. A part of a cow's head and a timber used in building.*

Caroline even used this tree-guessing activity at the Southern Forestry Congress.[31] Several foresters with the United States Department of

* The answers to the tree riddles are basswood, sweet gum, pine, beech (beach), cucumber tree, plane tree, ash, elder, and hornbeam.

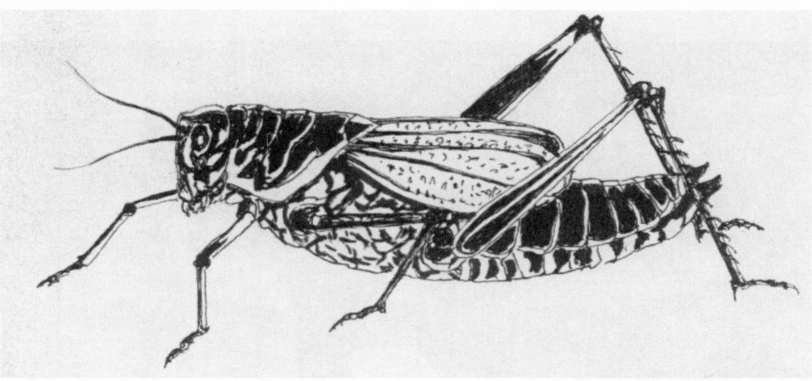

Courtesy Northwestern State University

Dormon's sketch of a grasshopper.

Courtesy Northwestern State University

Caroline Dormon as a young woman, ca. 1925.

Courtesy Northwestern State University

Caroline Dormon (center) at an autograph party for *Flowers Native to the Deep South,* ca. April 1958.

Agriculture wrote Dormon that they were impressed with the success of her methods of teaching forestry.

Dormon's favorite teaching method was blueprinting. Blueprinting was a tool for learning about leaves, fruits, and flowers. Dormon had refined a method that was simple enough for elementary school children. In later years, she wrote a narrative entitled "Blueprinting Nature," in which "The Tree-lady" teaches scouts the method by using ordinary items such as cardboard, glass, and clothespins. Blueprint paper and bichromate of potash were the only materials that had to be purchased.[32]

During the summer months, Caroline concentrated her teaching efforts at the State Normal at Natchitoches where teachers gathered. She frequently cited the German proverb "That which you wish to make a part of the nation, make it a part of the school system."

Caroline also prepared a bulletin entitled "Forest Trees of Louisiana: How to Know Them." It provided information about native trees and their value. The foreword suggests Carrie's perspective:

> Many of our native trees are far more attractive than some of those brought from other lands, and if these species were used more in planting, our parks and highways would take on an individual charm, typical of Louisiana alone. But this does not mean that promiscuous digging in the woods is to be indulged in. Shrubs and trees should never be removed from a roadside or camp-site.. . .
>
> Each individual in the state should feel a personal responsibility in preserving those of our trees which are in grave danger of being destroyed by the ruthless breaking of flowers and berries. It does not require close observation to see that dogwood, redbud, fringe tree, the berry-bearing hollies, and other highly ornamental species are rapidly disappearing from along highways and areas easily accessible to cities. It must be made a personal matter: 'I will *look and leave* and try to persuade others to do the same.'[33]

Carrie worked to see that the format of *Forest Trees* was attractive. When some in the Department of Conservation argued that the book should be pocket-size so that it could be more easily slipped into men's pockets, she countered that there were too many trees to keep it pocket-size and that women and children would also be using the bulletin. W. R. Hine, superintendent of forestry for the Department of Conservation, asked

Caroline to oversee every detail of the bulletin. He further credited Dormon with helping him to "get back a little bit of my appreciation of trees as trees."[34] The book was more than a success with over 30,000 copies distributed and an immediate need for a second printing.

Another early preservation operation initiated by Dormon was designed to "Save the Holly." Caroline sent information sheets to all federated clubs in the state, asking the members to place articles in local newspapers, give talks at schools and organizational meetings, and distribute "Save the Holly" stickers to motorists. Caroline was outraged at the greedy and capricious clipping of holly for Christmas decorations. Knowing that berry-bearing trees were few since the pistillate and staminate flowers are borne on separate trees, she wished to protect the holly from extinction. She did not demand abstention, but rather judicious and sparing clipping. She pleaded: "It is an appeal against ruthless destruction of one of the most beautiful trees of the forest. There are other adornments. Tearing or breaking off the limbs shortens their life, often killing them."[35] She even authored a poem to affirm the importance of saving the holly trees.

THE HOLLY SPEAKS
by
Caroline Dormon

Through fifty years of sun and storm I grew,
My urgent shoots thrust upward toward the light,
But never fast, adding yearly rings so slowly
My wood holds fast the secret of my age.

I won the fight, I held my own with those who would
have smothered me.
I reached the sun, attained my destined form.
Now I bear my lovely fruit—for what!
To be torn and cut and tossed away by wanton hands!

They say it is to make the Christmas bright.
Are not my berries brighter in the rain and sun?
They love the holly—so my graceful boughs are broken,
borne away.
To shine a few short hours and then to die.

Two years ago they cut away my perfect crown;
Patiently I sent my swiftest shoots to fill the emptiness.
Last year they left a gaping wound here in my side—
And now they come again with hatchets, axes, knives—

I keep the Yuletide spirit: my berries feed the hungry
birds,
Make pure the air which man defiles, my beauty give to
every asking eye.
For this my branches lie all mangled there,
My trampled berries blood-red in the snow.

Other evergreens were also being sacrificed for the Christmas season. Carrie implored:

> Plant your own Christmas trees . . . . Every year thousands of trees are cut down, beautifully decorated for a little while, and then thrown out to die. Why not plant a little everygreen in your yard and in a few years have a living Christmas tree.[36]

As chairman of forestry for the Louisiana Federation of Women's Clubs, Carrie sent out questionnaires to determine what was being done in the state for conservation. She wanted Louisiana to have credit for what was being accomplished, and she wanted to know what areas needed improvement. She publicized information about the accomplishments. In 1928 she boasted:

> Over four million acres of land were protected from fire last year. It is a joy to come to one of these protected areas, after driving for miles through burned-over-country. . . . Over half the wage earners in Louisiana are dependent for their support on the forest product industries.[37]

She knew that if fire-protection areas were to be increased, support would have to be gathered. She encouraged citizens to write their representatives and senators and other public officials urging that forest appropriations be increased, providing names and addresses for convenience. She issued letters to every "fellow club woman," explaining the funding of the Department of Forestry. She feared that the one fifth of the severance tax that the department was presently receiving was going to be re-routed to the general treasury, leaving the department absolutely dependent upon appropriations from the legislature. She felt that the club women had a "divine right"[38] to boost forestry, practically and aesthetically. She herself wrote numerous articles and letters. For example, in 1927 she wrote the editor of the *Plain Dealing Democrat* pleading for help in convincing landowners that "two cents an acre is a small price to pay for protection."[39] She wanted to see Louisiana return to being the leader in lumber production. She was certain that with forest protection and reforestation "every acre a producer" could become a reality.

In articles and in addresses, Dormon promoted her state, publicizing that Louisiana was the first state in the South to establish a division of forestry in the Department of Conservation. In the early twenties Louisiana had passed a full set of forestry laws which became a model for other Southern states as they later enacted laws of their own. Louisiana had been the first state in the nation to enact the "fifty-fifty" forest-fire protection whereby lumbermen and the state shared the cost of erecting fire towers and maintaining fire-fighting units. Louisiana was also one of the first states to establish a state forest nursery to distribute seedlings at cost to private landowners.

Carrie knew that a plan for "real reforestation" was essential. In an article for the Shreveport *Times* in August of 1927, her plea began with an Emersonian call:

> Let us not indulge in wild guesses and theories. . . . Let every thinking person find out what is being done. . . . Reforestation does not mean merely planting trees on denuded land, but also includes natural reforestation. In a short while every man and woman in Louisiana will be in possession of accurate information as to the wonderful possibilities of our state in the matter of timber productions. . . . It is a proven fact that Louisiana lands, if handled properly, will produce on an average 500 feet of pine lumber per year.[40]

Carrie's schedule was filled with personal appearances, speeches, and writing. In one year she made over twenty-six talks to various organizations and schools. "I put our stereopticon and slides in a Ford car and I am ready to carry forestry in a visible form to every school."[41] She was continuously adding to her slide and photograph collections, collections she used in her talks as well as loaned to others. She wrote bulletins for state parks and painted designs for calendars. Carrie was asked to identify the trees and shrubs in Audubon Park so that they could be permanently tagged.

Caroline literally worked day and night. She designed and implemented programs and activities, always looking ahead to reaching more people and teaching more nature subjects. Her work was noticed in and out of the state. Among those who took notice was Mississippi State Forester Roy L. Hogue:

> I have just returned from Asheville, yesterday, and heard again some very nice things about you, which make me more than ever eager to secure your services for our State if possible. I know of no one else to whom I should be willing to intrust this work, so if you fail me, I think that I shall abandon the idea of trying to have it done at this time. I believe that our Commission would be willing to pay almost any salary in reason for this work, because we consider it extremely important. So, name the salary that you think might induce you to come over into Mississippi and help us.[42]

In spite of this "name-your-salary" offer, Carrie's loyalty to Louisiana could not be purchased, and Carrie's dream of a national forest had not diminished.

In her capacity as supervisor of forestry education, she became acquainted with W. R. Hine, Louisiana state forester originally from New York. She showed Hine over all the impossible rocky roads of the area. He was, in Dormon's word, "enchanted" by the beautiful forest between Sandy and Odom's creeks. He had also been enchanted by the woman who had told of her fight to "save some of the beauty of the Kisatchie Hills in Natchitoches Parish."[43] He was impressed with her devotion and generosity, for at her own expense Dormon had taken any interested party across "barely passable roads." Hine too pledged his support. Hine, Ashe, and L. F. Kneipp, from the United States Forest Service, made a final inspection of the area and approved. Caroline thought: "I could relax at last, for my beloved Kisatchie was safe."[44]

But the wheels of the federal government slowed, for W. W. Ashe, who had wonderfully kept the project alive, died. Although the project languished, funds for the purchase had been appropriated. Caroline heard nothing of further progress. After pursuing many channels, Caroline wrote

Courtesy Northwestern State University

Dormon's sketch of her life as a forrester.

the director of the Southern Forest Experiment Station in New Orleans. He dispatched three foresters to the site that had been approved for purchase. Dormon took them out to inspect the area. On leaving, they assured her that she need not be concerned about the matter.

What followed, though, was a period of silence, then indifference, and finally blundering. The government had set aside $80.00 an acre for the virgin forest lands of Crowell-Spencer. Crowell-Spencer, however, was offerd only $12.00 an acre, an offer they could not accept. Soon logging engines puffed across Odom's Fall, and a magnificent and an irreplaceable forest was lost.[45]

Caroline must have felt that the years of effort she had expended to save the virgin forests were in vain; however, the first tracts of lands were purchased from Louisiana Long Leaf Lumber Company in late 1929, and with 76,589 acres of cutover land that would be reforested, the national forest became a reality on June 10, 1930. Carrie was given the opportunity to name the forest; appropriately, she designated it "Kisatchie," after its first inhabitants.

Although the virgin tracts of primeval forest had not been saved, Carrie's dream of forest lands had been realized. With that work completed and with a new political administration at the helm, Carrie wrote to W. R. Hine in 1929 to resign her forestry position.[46] Although she never again officially worked in state forestry, she had brought innovation to forestry education and preservation. The forestry profession honored her in 1930 by electing her an associate member of the Society of American Foresters.[47] She was the first female so elected.*

Notes

1. Caroline Dormon, typed letters to school principals in Louisiana, Caroline Dormon Colletion, Cammie G. Henry Research Center, Watson Memorial Library, Northwestern State University, Natchitoches, Louisiana, older 538.

2. *Ibid.*

3. P. H. Griffith, letter to Caroline Dormon, February 8, 1922, Folder 253.

4. Roy L. Hogue, Jackson, Mississippi, December 28, 1921, Folder 380

5. Caroline Dormon, typed notes, "The Story of Kisatchie," Folder 1092.

6. Bonnel H. Stone, letter to Caroline Dormon, May 17, 1922, Folder 381.

* Two other females were also elected at this time.

7. V. H. Sonderegger, letter to Caroline Dormon, April 7, 1922, Folder 385.

8. V. H. Sonderegger, letter to Caroline Dormon, September 12, 1922, Folder 360.

9. V. H. Sonderegger, letter to Caroline Dormon, June 24, 1923, Folder 361.

10. Caroline Dormon, letter to V. H. Sonderegger, August 19, 1923, Folder 361.

11. V. H. Sonderegger, letter to Caroline Dormon, August 23, 1923, Folder 361.

12. *Ibid.*

13. Caroline Dormon, letter to Dudley Berwick, August 15, 1923, Folder 361.

14. Dudley Berwick, Commissioner Department of Conservation, letter to Caroline Dormon, September 12, 1923, Folder 361.

15. Draft version of and notes relating to Enabling Act, Folder 1233.

16. Caroline Dormon, typed notes, "Federal Purchase of Forest Lands in Louisiana," Folder 1233.

17. Henry Hardtner, quoted by Caroline Dormon, typed notes, "The Story of Kisatchie," Folder 1092.

18. Debora Abramson, letter to Caroline Dormon, July 14, 1936, Folder 549.

19. V. E. Shelford, letter to Caroline Dormon, March 23, 1922, Folder 366.

20. W. W. Ashe, letter to Caroline Dormon, February 26, 1925, Folder 144.

21. W. W. Ashe, handwritten note, letter to Caroline Dormon, February 18, 1928, Folder 146.

22. Caroline Dormon, typed notes, "The Story of Kisatchie," Folder 1092.

23. Caroline Dormon, "The Kisatchie Wold," a wooden covered book made by Dormon and housed at NSU.

24. J. S. Crowell, letter to Caroline Dormon, February 24, 1922, Folder 398.

25. T. H. Harris, Circular No. 2420, January 28, 1928, Folder 355.

26. Caroline Dormon, typed notes for Tree Study, Folder 974.

27. R. D. Forbes, copy of a letter, Briarwood.

28. Caroline Dormon, typed notes on Forestry Essay Contest, Folder 362.

29. W. R. Hine, letter to Caroline Dormon, July 9, 1927, Folder 354.

30. Caroline Dormon, notes and book cover, Folder 356.

31. Caroline Dormon, notes on Tree-guessing Contest, Folder 1232.

32. Caroline Dormon, typed draft of "Blueprinting Nature," Folder 724.

33. Caroline Dormon, Forest Trees and How to Know Them, written under her title Assistant in Public Relations for the Division of Forestry in the Department of Conservation, Folder 757.

34. W. R. Hine, letter to Caroline Dormon, February 28, 1927, Folder 354.

35. Caroline Dormon, typed notes "Spare the Holly" and "Save the Holly," Folder 665.

36. Caroline Dormon, typed release for newspapers, Folder 667.

37. *Ibid.*

38. Caroline Dormon, typed letter to Federated Club members, Folder 667.

39. Caroline Dormon, typed letter to Editor of Plain Dealing Democrat, 1927, Folder 726.

40. Caroline Dormon, article for Shreveport Times, August 1927, Folder.

41. Caroline Dormon, quoted in The Atlantic Constitution, July 18, 1923, Melrose Scrapbook #83.

42. Roy L. Hogue, letter to Caroline Dormon, August 10, 1926, Folder 398.

43. W. R. Hine, letter to Caroline Dormon, September 2, 1958, Folder 408.

44. Caroline Dormon, "The Kisatchie Wold," a wooden covered book made by Dormon and housed at NSU.

45. Caroline Dormon, typed notes, "The Story of Kisatchie," Folder 1092.

46. Caroline Dormon, letter to W. R. Hine, February 27, 1929, Folder 358.

47. Folder 341 and Folder 382.

THE "IRISIAC"

Before 1920 only a few perceptive gardeners around New Orleans had noticed the multi-colored irises growing in the black muck-bogs and swamps along bayous, and only a few adventurous gardeners had attempted the daring task of collecting them. Dormon wrote of her own introduction to these "gypsy" beauties.

> No wild flower adventure can ever quite match my excitement on seeing them for the first time. In 1920 I was driving near Morgan City, in the coastal region of Louisiana, when I spied masses of giant iris growing in the ditch-banks. There were enormous flowers of various shades of lavender-blue, violet, and royal purple on stems four and five feet tall. Not only had I not seen such irises, but I had never even heard of them! When I got home, I rushed to my botanies—but no such species was described. At that time the only irises credited to Louisiana were little rush-red *Iris fulva, Iris hexagan*, with blue flowers over topped by foliage, and *Iris caroliniana*.[1]

Five years later, Dr. J. K. Small, curator of the New York Botanical Gardens, also saw these Louisiana irises. By the next year he had determined to learn more about the *Iridaceae*. In 1926, Dr. Small "discovered" the magnificent field of irises in New Orleans. During the next several years, he carefully explored the large field, collecting hundreds of different forms. He referred to the rich, wild iris fields of South Louisiana as the "Iris Center of the Universe."[2] Dr. Small named many of the irises and published information and paintings about them in *Addisonia*, the publication of the New York Botanical Garden. In a horticultural outing in 1926, Dr. Small visited Briarwood; he was surprised to find that the irises Dormon had brought back from that 1920 excursion were flourishing in her North Louisiana bog. Dr. Small presented Caroline a sack of rhyzomes, good varieties of blue and violet. When Caroline pleaded with him to tell her where she could secure whites and reds, he sent her to Mrs. B. S. Nelson. Mrs. Nelson and her sister Miss Ethel Hutson had been collecting and growing irises in their gardens for several years. Dr. Small introduced Dormon to others in the network of "irisiacs" in Louisiana, including George Thomas, a former superintendent of parks in New Orleans, who had discovered the first native yellow, a small Iris fulva in a bright aureolin shade; Mrs. Allen Ellender of Houma; Randolph Bezet and Joe G. Richard who went on expeditions with Dr. Small; Mr. and Mrs. Clifford Lyons, who upon leaving New Orleans gave their collection to Cammie Henry, who in turn shared with Caroline.[3]

Enchanted by this flower growing so well in natural bogs, Carrie, at first, collected almost indiscriminately because she was so excited to find the range of color and because she was experimenting to find which forms would succeed at Briarwood. (She was also collecting for Dr. Small.) Caroline and Cammie Henry made frequent collecting expeditions, Cammie's driver Fugaboo chauffeuring them to such places as Bayou Salé located near the gulf. The many varieties they found soon were at home at Melrose and at Briarwood where Carrie said they grew among asters, phystotegias, and "some real weeds."[4]

At Briarwood, Caroline planted and observed the irises. She did not consider her bogs an altogether fair testing ground inasmuch as Briarwood contained natural bogs with shade and coolness. She began giving plants to garden friends in various locations, locations which represented different types of soil and different weather conditions. She assiduously maintained records of the reports from these gardeners and visited the gardens so that she could draw conclusions about the iris.[5] She discovered that the iris had two requisities: generous water and food during the growing season. In addition, she found that the iris liked soil with plenty of humus and that iris in the Deep South liked full sun. Dormon not only shared her plants, she also shared her knowledge, corresponding extensively with fellow irisiacs and writing volumes of articles for newspapers and journals.

In the spring of 1932, Mary Swords Debaillon, an ardent gardener and naturalist, visited Briarwood to see Dormon. Mrs. Debaillon had first learned of Dormon through the articles Caroline had written on preservation of native flora. Mrs. Debaillon was already well known for her collection of camellias, azaleas, and magnolias. Now she wished to explore and collect native iris. She was particularly excited to find that the iris had adapted so well to the sand-hill streams. She and Caroline knew that this adaptability would enable the iris to become a garden flower. Caroline characterized this fellow naturalist as "a dainty women who tramped the bogs with men and spades."[6] Mrs. Debaillon knew no halfway measures; her collection, therefore, grew rapidly and beautifully.

During the first trip to Briarwood, Mrs. Debaillon was also captivated by Dormon's paintings for *Wild Flowers of Louisiana*. She asked Caroline to show her the native plants represented in the paintings. She carried many of the native sand-hill plants back to her own gardens in Lafayette. This was only the first of many exchanges. Dormon and Debaillon made many trips to the hills of North Louisiana and the bogs of South Louisiana.[7]

In 1937 W. B. MacMillan invited Mrs. Debaillon to explore some bogs near Abbeville where he had found wonderful reds and yellows. These were not only wonderful in color, but their form was also unique: the very broad sepals and petals were clawless, the style-arms were very short and quilled. Mrs. Debaillon wrote Carrie, telling her of the hundreds of huge reds and yellows and of the clones of them growing in massive clumps. She sent Carrie one plant of each of best varieties except for *Amazing* (later renamed *Homahoula*, Choctaw for "beloved red").

Mrs. Debaillon died in the spring of 1941, willing a large portion of her extensive iris collection to Dormon. Although Mary Debaillon had often spoken to her husband about this bequest, she also left him a written note specifically bequeathing the following to Carrie: "all my nature books and all iris north of the house to Caroline Dormon and also whatever wild-flowers she may select."[8] Carrie, though, had lost a friend. After Carrie paid tribute to Mary Swords Debaillon at the Iris Society meeting in 1942, Dan Debaillon wrote Carrie: "I do not believe anyone but you could have interpreted Mary as well as you did."[9]

In an effort to insure the continued perpetuation of these inherited plants, Dormon gave rhyzomes of each variety to the Southwestern Louisiana Institute of Lafayette, under the direction of Ira S. Nelson; to Louisiana State University at Baton Rouge; and to the newly formed Mary Swords Debaillon Louisiana Iris Society. The society was organized in Lafayette in May 1941. J. G. Richard, assistant extension horticulturist at LSU, sent Carrie a tentative charter for the organization so that she could make changes or suggestions.[10] Carrie helped promote the society, writing friends to "wear gloves, so you can get your hands 'pretty' before the iris meeting."[11]

Richard also asked Carrie's help in planting iris around the pond at Camp Grant Walker. Always instructive, Carrie advised Richard in the following way:

> I think it a lovely idea to plant the iris . . . but not those *rare* varieties. First, unless the caretaker guarded them with a machine-gun, someone would lift them when they bloomed. Mrs. Debaillon once had a clump of Thomas yellow, in bloom, lifted bodily out of her garden—and her at home! So what could you expect at an isolated camp? It is a curious trait of human nature that people who would not snitch so much as a pencil grab flowers from someone else! (My niece says she does not want to get interested in flowers because they weaken people's character!)[12]

Dormon was eager to observe the collection she had inherited from Mrs. Debaillon. The second year that she had the collection she was overwhelmed with the frilly white Jeune Fille, the huge rose-pink New Orleans, and the orchid bi-tone named for Mrs. Debaillon. The Debaillon plot produced only a few plants over three feet. Carrie preferred to have irises whose faces she could see whereas many irisiacs preferred irises that would grow to eye level. Nature cooperated with Carrie's plans for testing the irises. After a two-week period of summer-like heat, the temperature dropped to ten degrees. Carrie recorded that Haile Selassie, Peggy Mac, Bonrouge, Cajan, Reflected Light, Caroline Dormon, Gulf Sunshine, and Lillian Trichel survived and bloomed beautifully during the regular season. The following summer Nature provided a different test, a record-breaking drought. By this time Carrie had moved the Debaillon irises to a new garden with semi-shade and constant moisture. The original plot had contained no artificial watering facilities, but even the baked ground there produced some shoots.

Another survivor was Woodcarver's lavender-blue, a name Mrs. Debaillon used because she had found it near a woodcarver's house.[13] Carrie felt that garden iris should be named: "Who, pray, is going to remember B-6-41?"[14] She felt that numbers belonged to the hybridizer's plot, but varieties of merit, varieties of fine quality would get lost without names. Carrie had a test for a variety of merit: "If an iris has so much character that I can sit before my winter fire and evoke a clearcut mental picture of the flower, then that iris deserves a name by which it can be designated."[15] In an article for *Home Gardening*, she described some of her discoveries:

> Here in my sand hills, I have done a bit of hybridizing, and through sheer luck can claim some few without apology. (Most of mine go over the fence, as far as I can throw them!) *The Khan* is a lordly fellow, black-violet, with a headlight signal of bright yellow. It is a wonderful multiplier, which is unusual with the finest sorts. *Violet Ray* is even bigger, with seven-inch flowers of pansy purple, and cream rays extending out to center of sepal. It also has a tiny cream line around the edge of the entire flower. *Rose of Abbeville* is just what is says—an Abbeville iris in a warm rose color. I still love two of my old seedlings: *Saucy Minx*, with impudent ruffled flowers of brilliant rose-red; and *Candles*, amaranth, with picric yellow style-arms.[16]

Carrie referred to such hybridizing as "meddling with God's business."[17] She considered herself only the "veriest amateur" at hybridizing. She listed the origins of another of her hybrids June Cloud: "by the grace of God and the bees."[18]

Carrie had written The American Iris Society as early as 1935 to secure blanks for registering some of her varieties. She was careful to credit Mary Debaillon with the Debaillon irises. In most instances, Carrie used native names like Chacahoula. Indeed, she had such skill at appelations that friends prevailed upon her to name their irises. She continued collecting, wading "moccasin-infested" bogs and working from early morning until the dark of evening. "Today I put on galoshes and slushed down to the Beech Garden, and there were real buds! This is joy unalloyed—to watch graceful stems lift taller day by day each tipped with a slim green promise."[19] She diligently took notes, recording date and duration of blooms, measurements of flowers, floriferousness, fragrance, color, texture, variations in leaves, the seed pods, and weather endurance. These notes not only governed her own ongoing work with irises, they also were the raw material for Carrie's articles on irises.

Carrie's iris notes are so fresh and original that they often sound like poetry. In describing the color of a seedling, she queried "Can you recall the violet of a very vivid rainbow?"[20] On finding "a stray piece of heaven" (Ruth Dormon's Wood Violet), she exclaimed "the color is not of this earth."[21] She compared Wild Swan to its namesake: "The most enormous white I ever saw, with horizontal sepals and petals, but not too stiff to flap wild wings in the wind." She expressed the spectacle with "The show is on! the stage is filling."[22]

Carrie continued writing articles "poured right out of my experience."[23] In answer to a request, Carrie replied: "As to [the] article for A. I. S. Bulletin and the one for your yearbook, never fear, I can write both and not repeat myself. There is so much to say on the subject I could fill a volume."[24]

She also continued corresponding and trading with other iris enthusiasts, including professional botanists such as Dr. Small as well as W. B. Macmillian, Ira Nelson, Geddes Douglas of the American Iris Society, H. Senior Fothergill of London. By early 1932, a general public was writing Dormon, addressing her as "a well-known authority on iris." After reading an iris article by Dormon, one Californian who ardently wished to grow Louisiana irises wrote that Carrie was the only one who could help, and a physician from New York thanked Carrie for her generosity in sharing cherished seeds. Carrie established lifelong friendships with many of these enthusiasts. She often closed letters to these friends by quereing, "Isn't it fun?"[25] And it was Carrie who first provided a designation for these iris friends: "I call us irisiacs—like maniacs, you know!"[26]

Carrie was also sought out as a speaker on irises. She was eager to spread the glory of the Louisiana iris, but she was also mindful of her strength, readily stating that she "had a heart murmur." Her fees were moderate. For example, for a club lecture in Oklahoma, she charged a meager $60.00 for fee and automobile expenses. Frequently her sister Virginia accompanied her. Dormon generally requested that she not have to attend banquets and teas. She used her own slides of irises to illustrate her talks. When a group would ask her how long her lecture would be, she

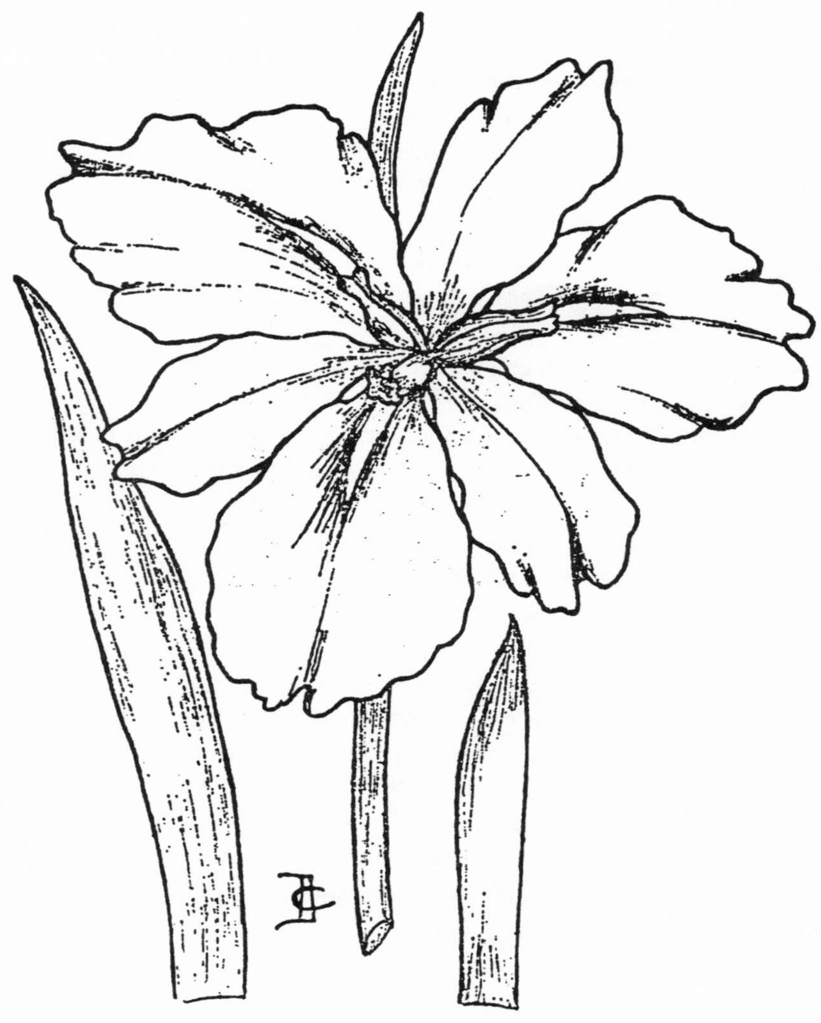

Sketch of an iris by Caroline Dormon.

replied: "Any length you desire! I can talk about these iris thirty minutes or thirty days!"[27]

Carrie and Virginia persuaded another enthusiast, their widowed sister-in-law Ruth Dormon, to grow and sell irises as a business venture. The business was aptly named Wild Garden. For almost a decade, the business grew and prospered. Carrie and Virginia continued the business after Ruth's death. Carrie was conscientious about the sales: selecting choice rhyzomes to send, including extra plants for "lagniappe, as we say in Louisiana—something thrown in,"[28] and writing detailed directions for planting and care. In answering a request from C. S. Milliken, of Milliken Gardens in Arcadia, California, Carrie explained the difficulty of continuing Ruth's business:

> Your letter of May 2nd would have been answered sooner, but I have been buried under an avalanche of people coming to see my iris. Mercy! They come from coast to coast. And I do NOT have a show place. I am growing these wonderful iris primarily to learn something about them. They constitute one of the great botanical mysteries—the unbelievable variations in size, form, and color.[29]

Carrie enjoyed discriminate visitors, extending invitations such as "I do not exactly 'open my garden,' but if you will write and make an engagement, I shall be happy for you and some of your friends to come."[30] What Carrie objected to was visitation that was inopportune, that happened when she had gardening, writing, or painting to do. These endeavors came with inherent time schedules, for Carrie had to paint when a flower bloomed. Carrie felt that indiscriminate visitors, tedious correspondence, demands of philistinistic buyers, and her health ("My heart is all right, so long as I do nothing! But who wants to do nothing—with flowers begging for attention?")[31] were unnecessary burdens of the business. She returned to her schedule: writing for magazines like *The Bulletin of the American Iris Society*; publishing almost annually a "Louisiana Iris Journal"; even contributing to international journals as far away as Australia and England; and, of course, growing flowers and painting.

All of this attention to irises was contagious, and the inevitable occurred. In a letter to Charles Gersdorff, chairman of The American Iris Society in the forties, Caroline expressed a concern:

Ap. 8-28 Delta Treasure
Ap. 8-29 "Hollyhock" (Fuchsia X Saucy) beaut., holds up well wonderfully
Ap. 8-28 "Wheel-horse" - lovely - 7 in., sep. 2¼ across -
8-27 Bordeaux Beauty - lovely color, too droopy
?-30 Kraemer Yellow. June F. -
Ap. 8-25 Acacia - holds up in rain!
Ap. 9-29 Ladies' Choice -
Ap. 10-23 "Gt. red giant" (Gypsy Q. X "wond. Ch. red.")
flrs. 7 inches (under crab, old garden)
holds up well, after rain
" 10-28 Susan-Moon
" 10-29 Jeune Fille
" 10-21 Dixie Deb. Op. 21
" 11-28 "black-red," beaut. color, leathery texture
" 11-26 New Orleans
" 11-28 Cameron White, lovely, sim. to W. Swan
" 11-25 Vineyard

Courtesy Northwestern State University

An entry from Caroline Dormon's iris notebooks.

Courtesy Northwestern State University

Caroline Dormon and Ira Nelson in the iris bogs at Briarwood.

> . . . The thing I have tried to do from the beginning, as I told you in my very first letter, is to keep the standard high on the checklist. If everyone had done this from the first, there would not now be *thousands* of names thereon! This multiplicity of names makes it practically impossible to tell what's what.[32]

She believed that seedlings should not prematurely be named and registered. "No one knows better than I that each introducer thinks his child is the fairest darling of all."[33] Yet she felt that introductions should be graded: "I [am] proud of my children! Unlike the human ones, I can throw away those that don't measure up."[34]

Another iris question about which Carrie and other irisiacs were concerned was that of species. Even by the end of the forties, no one had consistently studied and analyzed the question. Carrie knew that consistent study was the only way to amend the issue, and she was one of a few who had so studied. Carrie had read the ambiguous claims of botanists and amateurs. In fact, she was convinced that by the time the botanists worked the species out "most of us will have passed on to a land where irises do not have leaf-spot."[35] Her own preference was that the terminology should be Louisiana iris, not Louisiana hybrids, and she hoped that other Louisianians would not "supinely accept this misleading dumping."[36] She wrote Professor Sidney B. Mitchell of Berkeley, California, and Dr. L. F. Randolph of Cornell University, offering a rationale for Louisiana iris rather than Louisiana hybrids:

> . . . I am writing you relative to the misleading way in which the Louisiana irises are classified. . . . All Southern irises are dumped into one *sub-section*! Louisiana irises, the most remarkable addition taken as a group that has ever been contributed to the Iris Family, are not even given a *sub*-section. They are far more varied than the California group which is given a separate sub-section. . . . What I plead for is a cessation of the absurdity of calling *all* Louisiana irises "The Louisiana Hybrids." The California irises are not called "Cal. Hybirds,' so why ours, that range from tiny dwarfs a few inches tall, with button-seed-vessels, to six foot giants with fruits four inches long?[37]

Carrie also included in these pleas remedies for the classification issue. She suggested grouping Native Irises under the headings Hexagona, Fulva, Giganticaerulia, and Abbeville. Carrie recognized that the problem was more than a battle between the botanists and the horticulturists. She feared that plant politics and professional rivalry were adding to the ignorance and confusion of classification:

> . . . When I send in an iris to be registered, I do not know where to put it, for here is what I have to choose from: Fulva, Hexagona, and 'vinicolores.' That last means absolutely nothing. It even contradicts the 'damners'! Those who would throw out *all* Dr. Small's names did not accept I. vinicolor, so why turn around and make a group called 'vinicolores'?[38]

Carrie felt that she was being labeled an "objector, carrying on a one-man fight"; but her greater fear was that mistakes were being printed and, consequently, being accepted as facts.

Although Carrie did not singularly resolve the iris confusion, she brought knowledge of her own and inspired awareness in others. For such service The Society for Louisiana Irises, formerly Mary Swords Debaillon Louisiana Iris Society, of which Dormon was a charter member, voted Carrie winner of its 1948 award (Carrie had designed the medal for this award). Carrie served as judge for the American Iris Society, chair of the Bibliography Committee, honorary vice-president of the Spuria Society. She designed the seal for the American Iris Society. In addition to registering many irises including Easter Basket, Virginia, Rose Bells, Swan-Moon, Lady Storm, Persian Pink, Fire Alarm, and Upstart, Carrie won awards for the following irises: Violet Ray, The Khan, Wood Violet, Wheelhorse, and Saucy Minx.[39]

Carrie had not grown irises for awards or for praise, and she had not planted her gardens for a "show place." She had simply wished to share with the world the natural beauty of Louisiana iris. She succeeded. In her own words: "No longer is the Louisiana iris a wild Gypsy beauty, to be searched out among bogs and water moccasins. Our swamp debutante has become a horticultural queen."[40]

Notes

1. Caroline Dormon, "Louisiana Iris," The Garden Journal of the New York Botanical Garden, March-April 1953, Caroline Dormon Collection, Cammie G. Henry Research Center, Watson Memorial Library, Northwestern State University, Natchitoches, Louisiana, Folder 799.

2. Dr. J. K. Small, quoted in Louisiana Native Iris, Bulletin No. 1, p. 2, Folder 283.

3. Caroline Dormon, notes, Folder 748 and Folder 672.

4. Caroline Dormon, notes, Folder 672.

5. Caroline Dormon, Iris notebooks, Folder 328.

6. Caroline Dormon, "The Mary Swords Debaillon Iris Collection," Folder 809.

7. *Ibid.*

8. Mary Swords Debaillon, written instructions left to Dan Debaillon and forwarded in a letter to Caroline Dormon, April 13, 1940, Folder 47.

9. Dan Debaillon, letter to Caroline Dormon, April 20, 1942, Folder 47.

10. J. G. Richard, letter to Caroline Dormon, May 15, 1941, Folder 305.

11. Caroline Dormon, note at bottom of letter, March 26, 1946, Folder 325.

12. Caroline Dormon, letter to J. G. Richard, October 16, 1944, Folder 306.

13. Caroline Dormon, Mary Swords Debaillon Louisiana Iris Society, Bulletin 13, p. 4, Folder 283.

14. Caroline Dormon, Mary swords Debaillon Louisiana Iris Society, Bulletin 13, p. 7, Folder 283.

15. Caroline Dormon, Mary Swords Debaillon Louisiana Iris Society, Bulletin 13, p. 8, Folder 283.

16. Caroline Dormon, "Louisiana Iris Round-up," Home Gardening, July-August, 1951, Folder 802.

17. Caroline Dormon, letter to J. G. Richard, April 25, 1946, Folder 306.

18. Caroline Dormon, letter to Ike (Nelson), August 28, 1949, Folder 140.

19. Caroline Dormon, "Native Iris Journal, 1945," Home Gardening, July 1945, Folder 789.

20. *Ibid.*

21. *Ibid.*

22. Caroline Dormon, "Iris Journal, 1948," Home Gardening, September 1948, Folder 789.

23. Caroline Dormon, letter to Clarke Cosgrove, Alhaurbra, California, February 13, 1950, Folder 273.

24. Caroline Dormon, letter to Editor, New Zealand Gardener, March 1, 1947, Folder 150.

25. Caroline Dormon, letter to Dr. B. L. Von Jarchow, Racine, Wisconsin, July 25, 1945, Folder 105.

26. Caroline Dormon, Letter to Mrs. Lyon (Mildred), Van Nuys, California, February 1, 1949, Folder 94.

27. Caroline Dormon, letter to Mrs. Ora Whatoff, Oklahoma City, August 26, 1949, Folder 273.

28. Caroline Dormon, letter to Mrs. Lyon, February 1, 1949, Folder 94.

29. Caroline Dormon, letter to Mr. C. S. Milliken, Arcadia, California, May 18, 1947, Folder 121.

30. Caroline Dormon, letter to Mrs. Farmer, February 21, 1955, Folder 273.

31. Caroline Dormon, letter to Mrs. Eylar, July 20, 1948, Folder 69.

32. Caroline Dormon, letter to Chas. Gersdorff, c. a. 1946-1948, Folder 91.

33. Caroline Dormon, letter to Ira Nelson, May 14, 1945, Folder 139.

34. Caroline Dormon, letter to Mrs. Deal, April 25, 1945, Folder 34.

35. Caroline Dormon, typed notes titled "Southern Iris Species," Folder 125.

36. *Ibid.*

37. Caroline Dormon, Letter to Dr. L. F. Randolph, Cornell University, July 30, 1948, Folder 125.

38. *Ibid.*

39. Information from Folders 136, 238, 277, 350.

40. Caroline Dormon, "Louisiana Iris Round-up," Home Gardening, July-August 1951, Folder 802.

"FLOWER MISSIONARY"*

"I have to plant a few bulbs each fall—when I stop, you can say 'she's dead!'"[1] Although Carrie wrote this in a letter to a friend, she hardly confined her zeal for planting to bulbs. Indeed, it was her knowledge of and delight in many plants, rather than one or two species, that gained her an international botanical reputation and a vast network of flower friends.

Carrie rose daily at sunrise to work with her flowers. Her attire was a dress or a skirt and a blouse (she never wore pants), and she covered her head with a large, straw hat, often tied with a ribbon or embellished with a flower. Occasionally, she had help in the gardens, but she was selective with regard to her assistants. Even Virginia complained that Carrie must not have considered her I. Q. high enough to pull weeds.

With two natural running springs and aged humus, Briarwood provided the environment for growing a variety of plants. Further, Briarwood already contained a native collection: wild ferns, violets, phlox, fringed orchids, fragrant Indian pipes, masses of wild azalea, immense beech, and groves of pine. Carrie determined to add to this collection so that Briarwood would be a sanctuary of native Louisiana plants. This was an arduous undertaking inasmuch as Louisiana flora is varied.

Carrie was prepared for the undertaking, for she had always been a close observer of native plants. She merely continued this regimen. She maintained extensive notes on plant cycles, recording successions of blooms and details of outstanding performers and weather vicissitudes.

The weather was not always a friend to Briarwood native life, for Louisiana weather can be extreme in temperature and in precipitation. Summer often found Carrie at war with the elements: "We are burning up. I am killing myself watering. I vow I am going to quit—but when I see some rare plant dying, I just can't stand it." Carrie grieved: "It rains in circles all around me. . . . I get only sprinkles. The Lord must have turned me over to the devil 'for a season,' as he did poor old Job." But when the rains came, she rejoiced: "Aren't the rains delicious."[2]

* Dormon related the derivation of this name: "An old friend of mine—a college professor—used to call me a 'flower missionary' and I have never been called anything I thought nicer."[3]

The weather notwithstanding, Carrie continued adding to Briarwood by personal plant collecting, purchases, and gifts. For some of the purchases, Carrie sent seeds or plants rather than money. She sent premium quality seeds and plants; she expected the same. She had little time or money with which to be careless. When nursery personnel sent her inferior items, she expressed her distress. In a letter to a New Jersey salesperson, Carrie lamented the plants she received by characterizing them as "quite dead—the packing and soil around them were as dry as the Gobi Desert."[4]

In addition to planting new species at Briarwood, Carrie shared her information about native or rare plants with other botanists and gardeners. Dr. A. R. Kruckeberg, botanist at the University of Washington, wrote Dr. Lloyd Shinners at Southern Methodist University to inquire about *Silene subciliata*. Dr. Shinners replied that Caroline Dormon was "the only living soul who knows where *S. subciliata* grows."[5] Carrie had found it in one location in western Louisiana. She had plants that she had grown from seeds. When Dr. Kruckeberg asked Carrie to send him seeds or plants, she sent him three plants that she had raised from seeds. She told him that there would be more if the rabbits did not "LOVE 'EM."[6] In 1958 she shared some of her secret places with Dr. John A. Moore, Louisiana Polytechnic Institute (now Louisiana Tech University).

> You see I am interested not only in botany, but in conservation . . . you are sworn to secrecy by *me!* . . . *I* wanted you to know . . . for you look petty healthy, and will probably be with us for quite a while. While I may not be around too many years. You will think me selfish, but I have seen so many wildings destroyed by diggers.[7]

Carrie had discovered *eustylis purpurea*, too. Writing Dr. George Lawrence, Bailey Hortorium, Cornell University, she explained:

> My parents loved this little sand hill flower, but could not find it in a botany. Later, I could not find it. I painted it, and the first time Dr. Small and E. J. Alexander came to Briarwood, I showed it to them. They exchanged glances, and finally Dr. Small said, 'I never saw it before. Can you send bulbs to us at the Garden?'

Courtesy of
John C. Guillet

Caroline Dormon placing aluminum foil around a plant
to protect it from rabbits.

> This I did, and when they bloomed, Dr. Small wrote me that neither he nor any botanists who saw it had ever seen it before . . . . BUT Alexander wrote it up for *Addisonia—and* my name was not mentioned![8]

Edgar Anderson, curator of Useful Plants at Missouri Botanical Garden, though, recognized Carrie's botanical foresight. In the 1930s Anderson and a colleague were working with *Tradescantia.* Without knowing of their work, Carrie too was exploring the species. Intuitively, she sent them unsuspected species from southern Louisiana, *Tradescantia paludosa.* Anderson and other scientists throughout the world used this plant in radiation research.

Another plant intrigued Carrie: a new species of the common spider-lily or *Hymenocallis.* She submitted the new species to many plant authorities, with the plea: "If someone does not work out our own Hymenocallis, I am going to run off and start gnawing the bark off trees."[9] To Dr. Small she sent plants of the autumn or late summer blooming form. He identified it as *H. occidentalis,* the name traditionally given to the spring flowering form. Carrie rejected this nomenclature, for she had observed other differences between the forms: namely the greater variation in the spring varieties, some with giant flowers and some that did not multiply. She had read the botanies and knew that it was not recorded, but none would recognize her discovery. Again, she would not be credited with "discovery." Dr. Lloyd Shinners was given credit, and he named the plant *Hymenocallis eulae* for Eula Whitehouse.

Carrie did not crusade for plants to be named after her, but she did, with zeal, insist on credit for Louisiana. She chastised Dr. Edgar Wherry, eminent botanist from the University of Pennsylvania.

> When did you fall out with Louisiana?? I was much interested in an article on phloxes (by you in *Horticulture*, I think), but was amazed to see that you had stricken Louisiana from the list! Don't you remember the masses of the phlox you call P. pilosa ozarkana at Ruth Dormon's? And don't you remember the P. divaricata I took you to see at Ft. Humbug (Shreveport), the one you said had the broadest leaves you ever saw? And I sent you specimens of P.

> Glaberrima from a number of sites in the state. Remember the plumbago blue (*almost*) one you saw blooming here at Briarwood? And have you forgotten our collecting P. divaricata on a creek below here. . . .[10]

In fact, Dr. Wherry had come to Louisiana in 1934 to study the species because Carrie had sent him specimens that had not been listed in the botanies. Carrie guided Wherry to native beds of phlox. Determining that the phlox had not been previously identified, Wherry and two geologists returned in 1936. At that time he asked Carrie's help in acquiring specimens of *Dryopteris ludoviciana,* a fern recorded by early explorers but then viewable only at the Berlin herbarium.[11]

Carrie too had a collection of dried plant specimens: "My 'herbarium' is an unholy mess, many things stacked between newspapers in my attic."[12] Yet specialists such as W. W. Ashe and John Small frequently asked for her help in identification. Although she did not always know the plant, she knew what it "ain't!"

Carrie corresponded with other prominent plant scholars throughout the United States. Dr. George H. M. Lawrence, director of the L. H. Bailey Hortorium, requested plants and specimens. He even asked her to respond to some of the correspondence he received. For example, when Mrs. L. Roy Brace wrote to ask about the derivation of Confederate Jasmine, Dr. Lawrence replied: "I suggest that you write Miss Dormon, who recently published the finest book on wildflowers of the deep south that I know of and ask her if she has any information on it."[13]

Donald Wyman, horticulturist at the Arnold Arboretum, was another specialist who exchanged letters and plants with Carrie. In 1944 Carrie wrote Wyman: "I have tried for over twenty years to be a sort of missionary in getting people interested in our fascinating native flora. It has been a long, slow job, but at last there is an awakening."[14]

Through her writings and letters and generous donations of plants and specimens, she succeeded in awakening a number of botanical societies to the flora of Louisiana, including the New York Botanical Garden, the New York State Museum, Charleston Museum, the California Academy of Sciences, the Brooklyn Botanic Garden, Arnold Arboretum, University of Florida, Southern Methodist University, University of North Carolina,

Mills College, Washington University, Harvard University. All of these (and numerous others) requested and received plants and information from Dormon. Dwight M. Moore, University of Arkansas, credited Carrie's donation of three bulbs of *Eustylis* as the beginning of "a chain of events which leads to this new record for the State,"[15] for when Carrie's bulbs bloomed, he realized that he previously identified the flower incorrectly as *Nemastylis*.

In 1929, the United States Department of Agriculture solicited Carrie's cooperation in finding plant information "for the use of the Government as a measure of national preparedness."[16] W. W. Eggleston of the Department of Agriculture requested that Carrie identify plants that might provide medicinal value as well as the locations where such plants grew. Eggleston also inquired about which plants were collectible in commercial quantities.

Thomas Edison, too, asked for Carrie's assistance. Dr. John Small had told Edison that Carrie grew goldenrod at Briarwood. In June of 1930, Edison wrote to enlist Carrie's help in securing specimens of various kinds of goldenrod, for he was experimenting with the plant as a potential source of rubber. For over a year, Carrie collected leaves and seeds and roots. Edison shared with Carrie the results of his experiments.[17]

Carrie's correspondence and plant exchanges were international. H. Senior Fothergill of the Iris Society of London and Carrie exchanged seeds and plants and information. Fothergill even sent Carrie draft versions of articles so that she could purge them of "Englishism."[18] Carrie supplied the Royal Botanic Gardens at Kew with seeds of various plants. She also sent seeds to Lord Aberconway of Denbighshire. The majority of seeds Carrie sent were of native Louisiana plants. She sent birdfoot violet plants and dwarf iris to Japan and to New Zealand. Briarwood literally blooms around the world. These international friends reciprocated, for Briarwood received many new and rare plants.

Although Carrie responded to requests of major botanical societies, she also spent much time helping friends and neighbors with identification. Often a letter to Carrie simply contained a crumpled leaf and a plea. Carrie's response generally provided identification, information, and encouragement. In a letter to G. M. Snellings, Monroe, Louisiana, she wrote:

Cable Address "Edison, New York"

From the Laboratory
of
Thomas A. Edison,
Orange, N.J.

June
twenty-seventh
1930

Miss Caroline Dormon,
Chestnut,
La.

My dear Miss Dormon:

Our mutual friend, Dr. John K. Small, of the Botanical Garden in New York, informs me that you have a lot of goldenrod growing in your reservation, and has intimated that you would probably send me a sample on request.

Same would be very acceptable, and I would ask that you kindly send me about 2 grams of the leaves of the goldenrod (Salidago) after the flowers have closed and the seed is ripening.

Thanking you in advance for your courtesy, I remain

Yours very truly,

Thos A Edison.

Each Kind of Golden rod.

Ediphoned-C

E

Courtesy Northwestern State University

A copy of the June 27, 1930, letter from Thomas A. Edison to Caroline Dormon.

> The shrub is Sophora secundiflora, 'Texas mountain laurel.' When I talked to the garden clubs in Dallas, I laughed at them for tacking the word 'Texas' to everything. This is no relation to the true Mountain Laurel, *Kalmia latifolia*. 'Bush wisteria' would be a more appropriate name for the Sophora, as the racemes of lavender-blue pea-shaped flowers are not unlike those of wisteria, and, of course, they belong to the same family.
>
> . . . This is one of the slowest-growing shrubs I know. . . . But the plant is worth waiting for. Without a blossom, it is an attractive evergreen; and when hung with the racemes of blue-lavender blossoms, it is lovely.[19]

Carrie had many "flower friends." Among them was Mrs. Oscar Shanks. Mrs. Shanks had told Carrie of a location where Stuartia grew. In thanking her for sharing the "find," Carrie wrote: "If you had sent me a rope of pearls or a diamond tiara, you would not have made me half so happy."[20] Carrie also wrote Mrs. Shanks to warn her of prematurely letting the public know of the plot: "Persons who are otherwise upright and respectable citizens seem to have no code of ethics in the matter of despoiling wild flowers and trees."[21]

Plants were even Carrie's therapy: "Yesterday I dug among my flowers a few hours. That cures all my ills." Flowers truly raised her spirits: "Oh, I feel so *elevated*. At last I have coaxed a hepatica to bloom for me."[22] Flowers offered some rationality to modern life: "A flower open on Iris bakeriana. . . . And one blossom on N. b. foliosa. . . . These things make life possible—with Kruschev [*sic*] and Castro in the same world."[23]

Carrie often addressed her flowers: "Oh you darling little thing! You're going to bloom at last!"[24] The trees and shrubs and flowers provided her joy.

> I picked my first violets *today—viola villosa*. Insignificant though it is, there is something especially dear about this little violet. The flowers are small and have very short stems, but they are delicately fragrant. And it is always the first to come—our very first wildflower, unless you count the yellow catkins of the tag-adler.[25]

The variety of plants that Carrie had knowledge of was vast, but at various times she expressed particular preferences for certain plant attributes. First, she preferred fragrance. The perfume of crabapples was a favorite, and Carrie planted them all over Briarwood.[26] Another fragrant favorite was Indian pipes.

> I feel sure our Indian pipe is a different species from the northern one. Ours always blooms beneath pines, the northern one beneath hardwoods. Ours is very fragrant (this is how I locate them); all botanies say the northern one is 'scentless.' Theirs blooms in summer, ours in late fall. There is some difference in form.
>
> Oh, strange flower, that grows like a fungus from decaying vegetable matter; which has no color; but which is a true flower and bears seeds. But with all your strangeness you are a lovely and lovable forest sprite. I love the name the little sand-hill children give them, 'frost pipes.'[27]

In a letter to Dr. Lawrence, Carrie described the scent of *Spiranthes odorata*: "I will not say 'vanilla scented'! You men! You have things smelling like allspice, etc. when none of these things can compare in sweetness with the perfumes of flowers."[28] Carrie felt that scents of plants were not always accurately described since many botanists relied on dried specimens.

She also liked shrubs with small leaves.[29] In describing Cyrilla, one of her favorite shrubs, Carrie wrote:

> The fluffy flowers come after our summer weather has arrived. And right now, there are many glistening red leaves among the green. It blooms when not more than 3 feet in height, though eventually becoming 15 or even 20.[30]

Carrie's choice of color was white or delicate shades; for example, she considered the azalea George Lindley Tabor "the most beautiful one of all."[31] Yet she was delighted by deep darks, especially reds.

With regard to roses, she had various opinions. She was not fond of York and Lancaster because it was "variegated, not STRIPED."[32] In fact, she exclaimed: "I don't like variegated plants—they look to me as if they have a virus!"

Although Carrie preferred that flowers remain growing naturally, she occasionally picked some blooms to bring inside. Carrie compared one of her bouquets of daffodils to pictures in the Wayside catalog. Carrie's love of plants was so vast that she often expressed that love in hyperbole. Of *M. robusta persicifolia* she wrote: "I think if I do not see one bear before I die, I cannot be quite easy in my grave."[33]

Such passion and knowledge had to be shared. She was unselfish and undaunted in forwarding her flower opinions. She wrote A. J. Hodges when he began formulating plants for Hodges Gardens in Many, Louisiana. Hodges Gardens was, like Briarwood, located in sand hills. Carrie hoped that Hodges would make the garden more than "millions of camellias and azaleas" and less than a mob attraction with golf courses and "other foolishness."[34] She unassumingly offered her point of view: "I know you must chuckle over the women wanting to give you free advice."[35] Hodges, though, wanted her perspective and soon wrote to ask if he could visit her gardens. She replied: "Let me hasten to disabuse your mind of the idea that I have 'gardens'! I have 120 acres of wildwood . . . I do have many rare and beautiful things—but often you have to look through the briars to see them!" Carrie was eager to share her knowledge and even her plants with Hodges. After visiting with Carrie, Hodges hired her as "Consultant on Natural Areas," paying her one hundred dollars a month. Immediately she began surveying the areas for natural gardens, ordering plants, and instructing the workers. Although Carrie worked only one year in this capacity, she continued to make contributions to Hodges Gardens. On one occasion Hodges discovered that she had gone to the gardens and planted some of her Louisiana iris and scattered wildflower seed. He forwarded her a check, but she returned it, noting "you did not ask for them."[37]

Throughout her life, Carrie encouraged many others to grow plants, always explaining the prerequisites of gardening.

> I hate to explode all the lovely old theories about green thumbs, magic fingers, and all other fairy gifts, but successful

> gardening actually comes down to such earthy matters as elbow-oil and stout back and everlasting persistence. Keen observation is essential. And of course love does come into it—unless you truly love growing things, just plant a few shade trees, put in a nice lawn, and stop right there. Keeping them in shape will give you enough outdoor exercise. But leave the sweet agony of gardening to the possessed ones.
>
> Of course gardening is a virulent disease and highly contagious, and often the most unexpected victim will come down with it. I often think these inexperienced ones have the most fun of all, for they have to run the full gamut of agonizing mistakes, failures, etc., but when success does crown their efforts, their pride is a touching thing. A crowned head achieving a royal heir could not be more exultant.[38]

Carrie knew well the sweet agonies and the unparalleled reward of gardening.

Notes

1. Caroline Dormon, letter, April 25, 1968, on display at Briarwood.

2. Caroline Dormon, letter, Caroline Dormon Collection, Cammie G. Henry Research Center, Wastson Memorial Library, Northwestern State University, Natchitoches, Louisiana, Folder 1016.

3. Caroline Dormon, letters, Briarwood.

4. Caroline Dormon, letter to Rex D. Pearce, Moorestown, N. J., November 16, 1954, Folder 107.

5. Dr. Lloyd Shinners, quoted by D. A. R. Kruckeberg in letter to Caroline Dormon, September 20, 1957, Folder 161.

6. Caroline Dormon, letter, Briarwood.

7. Caroline Dormon, letter to Dr. John A. Moore, February 8, 1958, Folder 89.

8. Caroline Dormon, letter to Dr. George Lawrence, Cornell University, Folder 56.

9. Caroline Dormon, letter to Edgar Anderson, Missouri Botanical Garden, May 29, 1957, Folder 419.

10. Caroline Dormon, letter to Dr. Edgar Wherry, July 8, 1946, Folder 247.

11. Information from Folders 246 and 749.

12. Caroline Dormon, note, on display at Briarwood.

13. Dr. George H. M. Lawrence, L. H. Bailey Hortorium, letter forwarded to Caroline Dormon, January 22, 1959, Folder 56.

14. Caroline Dormon, letter to Donald Wyman, Arnold Arboretum, November 17, 1944, Folder 186.

15. Dwight M. Moore, University of Arkansas, letter to Caroline Dormon, July 20, 1955, Folder 87a.

16. W. W. Eggleston, United States Department of Agriculture.

17. Thomas A. Edison, letters to Caroline Dormon, dated June 17, 1930, July 22, 1930, December 11, 1930, February 2, 1931, Folder 262.

18. H. Senior Fothergill, London, letter to Caroline Dormon, September 11, 1947, Folder 150.

19. Caroline Dormon, letter to Dr. G. M. Snellings, April 15, 1943, Folder 248.

20. Caroline Dormon, letter to Mrs. Oscar Shanks, n.d., Briarwood.

21. Caroline Dormon, letter to Mrs. Oscar Shanks, August 15, 1932, Briarwood.

22. Caroline Dormon, letter to Mrs. Edgar Stern, January 27, 1947, Folder 266; Caroline Dormon, typed journal entry, February 7, 1937, Folder 977.

23. Caroline Dormon, letter to Elizabeth Lawrence, January 21, 1961, Elizabeth Lawrence Collection, #28.

24. Caroline Dormon, quoted by Al Alleman, Morning Advocate Magazine, October 31, 1954.

25. Caroline Dormon, typed journal entry, January 17, 1937, Folder 977.

26. Caroline Dormon, letter to R. J. Wilmot, August 2, 1946, Folder 216.

27. Caroline Dormon, typed journal entry, October 1, 1937, Folder 977.

28. Caroline Dormon, letter to Dr. George Lawrence, September 4, 1957, Folder 1257.

29. Caroline Dormon, letter to Sam Rix, New Zealand, December 12, 1954, Folder 317.

30. Caroline Dormon, letter to W. M. Campbell, Director of Kew Gardens, London, January 1951, Folder 151.

31. Caroline Dormon, letter to Mrs. Witherspoon, March, Folder 217.

32. Caroline Dormon, letter addressed "My dear," August 19, 1969, on display at Briarwood.

33. Caroline Dormon, letter to Donald Wyman, June 18, 1942, Folder 86.

34. Caroline Dormon, letter to A. J. Hodges, September 5, 1956, Folder 172.

35. Caroline Dormon, letter to A. J. Hodges, April 3, 1955, Folder 171.

36. Caroline Dormon, letter to A. J. Hodges, January 13, 1955, Folder 171.

37. Caroline Dormon, letter to A. J. Hodges, December 27, 1956, Folder 172.

38. Caroline Dormon, typed manuscript titled "Nobody Knows the Trouble I See," Folder 825.

Courtesy Northwestern State University

Members of the De Soto Commission appointed by President Franklin D. Roosevelt.

"DE SOTOIZING"

Whereas we are approaching the four hundredth anniversary of the expedition of Hernando De Soto, the first and most imposing expedition ever made by Europeans into the wilds of North America; and

Whereas it is desired that this four hundredth anniversary of that great expedition be properly celebrated and markers placed at such points along the route of said expedition as may be definitely determined and established after thorough investigation; and

Whereas it is necessary to have a committee or commission to make a proper study and report back to Congress its recommendations for such a celebration: Therefore be it Resolved by the Senate and the House of Representatives of the United States of America in Congress assembled, That the President of the United States be, and he is hereby, authorized to appoint a commission consisting of not fewer than five nor more than seven members, to make a thorough study of the subject of De Soto's expedition and to report back to the next session of Congress its recommendations for a suitable and appropriate celebration of the four hundredth anniversary of said expedition.[1]

The above resolution was approved on August 26, 1935, by the United States Commission and funded in February of 1936. President Franklin D. Roosevelt appointed the members of the commission: W. G. Brorein, Tampa, Florida; Caroline Dormon, Chestnut, Louisiana; John R. Fordyce, Hot Springs, Arkansas; Andrew O. Holmes, Memphis, Tennessee; V. Birney Imes, Columbus, Mississippi; Walter B. Jones, Tuscaloosa, Alabama; and John R. Swanton, Washington, D. C.[2]

Caroline not only was selected to represent Louisiana, she was also the only female appointed to this commission. She was not, though, a token of female representation. For years she had engaged in extensive study of early American inhabitants and explorers.[3] She had corresponded with others who shared these interests, exchanging ideas and materials. In 1932 Dormon had written Dr. John R. Swanton, head of the Bureau of Ethnology at the Smithsonian Institution, concerning the route of De Soto. Swanton found her theories interesting and plausible. Dormon had already begun formulating hypotheses about the route of De Soto. She was convinced that the route was not as apparent as some assumed. She knew that part of the difficulty in determining a route was that the course of waterways, in particular the Mississippi River, had changed over the four hundred years since De Soto made his journey. Caroline had also helped Dr. Swanton locate some of the salt springs which De Soto had visited. For almost a decade Swanton and Dormon had swapped ideas to such an extent that Swanton coined words in a 1932 letter to Dormon to designate their fascination: "to DeSoto—the enterprise of tracing his route; to DeSotoize—to convert unsuspecting amateurs to the game."[4] Knowing of her knowledge of and interest in ethnology and archaeology, Swanton himself recommended that Dormon be appointed to the commission.

At the initial meeting of the De Soto Commission held March 5 to 7, 1936, in Washington, D. C., John R. Swanton was elected chairman, and Colonel John R. Fordyce was elected vice-chairman. A fact-finding committee was also elected. Swanton, Fordyce, and Dormon were elected to serve on the committee. Caroline suggested that the committee secure the Spanish documents that related to the exploration and have them translated.[5] Caroline envisioned an identified route that would allow visitors "to drive comfortably over the entire journey made by the Spanish army of exploration."[6] She felt that permanent exhibits should be arranged "to house artifacts, handcrafts, pictures, etc. to depict the original Indian life of the locality."[7] Caroline knew that the Indians had played an important part in the explorations of De Soto. She further suggested that pageants be given to reenact the historical occurrences along De Soto's journey. Such reenactment would, she believed, afford historical celebration as well as involve local participants, especially Indians. She spoke of the effectiveness of similar pageantry: "At the Natchez Pilgrimage, the women dress in antebellum costumes every day for about ten days . . . and consider it fun."[8]

Early in the commission's work, Caroline realized the inherent political problems. Even in Louisiana there were those who were politically trying to be placed on the commission although Caroline had earned her appointment. In some letters Caroline refers to one such jealous intriguer, a "Mr. E."[9] There were also those whose greatest concern was to have the De Soto route and markers in certain places for personal reasons. Dr. Swanton, too, feared that some people would act out of personal or political motivation. He wrote Caroline: "I am moved by the recent receipt of copies of Col. Fordyce's selection of towns to be honored by De Soto markers to say that you and I will have to exert something of a restraining influence on our colleague on the fact-finding committee."[10] Caroline wrote Fordyce, asking that he not be hasty in concluding a De Soto route, for she had done extensive work on the Louisiana portion. Swanton and Dormon both believed that Fordyce was too quick to accept a route as authentic. Because Fordyce had secured appropriations from Arkansas to place markers along the De Soto route through Arkansas, he wanted the commission to endorse the sites so that he could place the markers early. The main argument of Fordyce seemed to be that he had the money for the markers; Swanton and Dormon were, on the other hand, primarily concerned with the authenticity of the route and the accurate placement of the markers.

In fact, Dormon was vigilant in guarding against the release of premature theories. Carrie read closely the reports and correspondence of the other committee members, correcting and amending when necessary. Her letters frequently contained subtle instructions. In a letter to Col. Fordyce she remarked: "I think your idea of three different types of celebration is an excellent one. . . . Of course, I understand that the list you sent is not to be made public, but is just for discussion by the commission. And it will be very convenient to have your list for reference when the discussion takes place."[11]

Caroline did not seek nor want publicity or social regard. She carefully avoided those who wanted to scoop the commission. From time to time she and other commission members were invited to be guests at social gatherings. In most instances Carrie viewed these gatherings as impediments. She wrote Col. Fordyce to enlist his help in declining such invitations.

> Now all this is very nice, but you know a whole crowd cannot accomplish very much *work*. Another thing, we want anything BUT publicity until we get our theories at least half-baked. And you know those people from . . . will have a big blurb in their paper—and then all others will follow . . . Our friends will take it as entirely all right if you gently suggest that they have the

> proposed supper or other get-together a little *later—after* we have worked over the route in that region a little.[12]

The commission held its second meeting in Tampa, Florida, from May 4-6, 1936. The members spent much of the time in Tampa examining the region where De Soto landed. At this meeting Dr. Swanton made a progress report from the fact-finding committee, and Mr. Holmes presented information about previous celebrations conducted by the United States. The members left Tampa to return to their respective commission concerns. They met again in December at the University of Alabama at Tuscaloosa, Alabama. Dr. Swanton shared his committee's activities. The committee had secured the help of Miss Irene A. Wright, then a resident in Seville. Miss Wright had a knowledge of the collections in the Archivo General de Indias, the main archives of Spanish-American documents in the Iberian peninsula, and had done research in the libraries of Madrid, Jerez de los Caballeros, De Soto's birthplace, and other localities.[13] The fact-finding committee secured a translation of Garcilaso de la Vega's *La Florida*. The 910 type-written page story told of the Florida invasion.[14] The committee utilized maps from the Bureau of Soils, War Department, Coast and Geodetic Survey, and the Geological Survey in order to identify and verify the geographical route of De Soto. In addition, members of the Commission devoted several weeks to a direct examination of the country over which De Soto's group passed. During one such examination, the committee members seemed to disagree about the time it would have taken De Soto to travel a particular distance. Caroline suggested that a reenactment by the committee would have greater validity if the committee journeyed on foot rather than by car. She finally convinced the other members that even a reenactment on foot would be dissimilar, for De Soto's men, she argued, wore "cast-iron underwear."[15] They agreed, and much of the territorial examination was, thus, done on foot. Not only was this kind of examination more realistic, Caroline, no doubt, also enjoyed the opportunity for close inspection of the flora of the various geographical areas.

Carrie continued seeking information about the route of De Soto, writing various government agencies and university departments. In particular, Carrie sought information about waterways; she hypothesized that present rivers did not run as they had run four hundred years earlier when De Soto first explored the area. The following letter to a regional officer in the United States Engineer's Officer was an inquiry about such possibility.

> Is it probable that the Ouachita left its present channel below Live Oak Landing, followed one of the old channels to and through Lake Cocodrie, thence to the Mississippi through the channels previously indicated?
>
> Or would it have been possible for the Ouachita to reverse the present current of the lower Tensas, flowing eastward to Brushy Bayou, following the present channel of Brushy to the present Caney Bayou and Turtle Lake, through Black Bayou, and into the Mississippi just below Ferriday?
>
> Could the Tensas River had left its present channel near Dunbarton, flowed south through one of the old channels, through Shanty Lake, through another old channel which passed by the two Baptist Churches on Indian mounds, thence into Caney Bayou, and Turtle Lake, and into the Mississippi just below Ferriday?[16]

In addition to the river issue, Dormon was interested in other De Soto questions. Dormon concentrated on certain river crossings such as the crossing of the Red River by Luis de Moscoso, De Soto's successor. Carrie was chauffeured by Virginia whose teaching duties were measured in total hours rather than fixed time frames. Virginia also knew the roads better than Carrie. With Virginia driving, Carrie was free to observe and to take notes. They journeyed many miles along swamp country, attempting to follow the wanderings of De Soto's army. Most of these journeys were at their own expense. Although Carrie was authorized to claim five cents a mile when she used her car and five dollars a day when she was away from home, her total expenditures could not exceed fifty dollars.

Sister and Carrie explored saltworks for Dr. Swanton. Carrie forwarded the findings to him, sometimes suggesting her own conclusions, sometimes asking him to draw conclusions.

> I think Sister and I have checked off another saltworks. It was an interesting trip in the Spanish Sabine River country. . . .

> Though, we found no signs of Indian salt-making, this could easily have been called 'The Place of Salt,' for there are miles and miles of licks and strange little clear, deep lakes, with high banks—water faintly salt. If the people of Naguatex were encountered higher up, and on the Red River, I still think they came originally from Sabine River and vicinity. We learned of other salines lower down, and I think we will find salt-making signs there.
>
> After that, I have two other salines to investigate, and then you can just take your choice. . . .
>
> I forgot to say that we could not convince the Sabines that we were not treasure-hunters.[17]

Carrie conjectured that *Naguatex* and *Natchitoches* could be the same. She presented her theory to Swanton:

> Give the final *x* in *Naguatex* an *sh* sound, as in *Uxmal*, and you have something perilously close to *Nakatosh—it* would have been an easy matter for the Spaniards to have turned *Nawatosh* (or probably *Nawatesh*) into *Nakatesh—most* people really pronounce it that way.
>
> If it means 'the place of salt,' the Province of Naguatex could easily have contained the parishes of Natchitoches and Sabine, both of which were filled with salt licks and springs. . . .
>
> Last night, I came across a sentence in Garcilaso that seems to simply rivet it down. . . . On page 639, while the Spaniards were at Autiamque, he has De Soto and soldiers go on a foray to Naguatex, only 20 leagues away. They capture some Indians and return. This is just the right distance from Autiamque (Camden?) across to the upper Natchitoches town on the Red River. Later, page 641, he says they marched to Naguatex, but *not the same* as that which the Governor went to on his recent foray! Have you already observed this significant satement?. . .
>
> Also, it has always seemed odd to me that there should have been two Natchitoches towns so far apart. Surely the Province of Naguatex was not *that* large.[18]

While Swanton did not agree with Carrie's Natchitoches theory, he did agree with other theories she postulated. In October of 1936, he wrote her that he had finished a rough draft of his findings on De Soto:

> I am now prepared to go back over it and tear it up. A considerable struggle with the Ouachita River has convinced me that you are right about the crossing place and that it was at Columbia.[19]

On this issue, Carrie had argued that the army would not have crossed the Ouachita only to cross back over, that no mounds had been found to substantiate claims by researchers such as Elvas, that the army had built a town on the low ground of the Boeuf, and that the journey time was right for a crossing at Columbia. The Columbia crossing decided, Carrie attended other concerns: mixed-up bayous and unaccountable wanderings and unexplainable time lapses. Again she approached Swanton with her beliefs.

> Just as you consent to allow them to cross at Columbia, I jump Nilco up to Sicily Island! I know you will say *that* is *too* much. But it sticks in my mind like a burr—I am worrying it down. For example, why did they cross the Ouachita, apparently just for pleasure of marching through terrible swamps?. . . It is perfectly possible, it seems to me, that the Ouachita ran much nearer the bluff on the east side of Sicily Island at that time, which would have placed it much nearer the mound I selected at Nilco.[20]

Carrie made other trips and continued reading previous accounts to support the Sicily Island theory. Previous accounts had described the place as looking down on a level plain and as a country with abundant maize. The Peck plantation on the southeast side of Sicily Island fit the description. She also found the corn in Sicily Island superior to the corn grown in Jonesville. Examining the soil, she discovered the soil in Jonesville as "tight, craw-fishy, and not corn land at all."[21] She parenthetically asked Swanton if he had known she was such an expert farmer.

Carrie's very nature was inquistive. She observed, she read, she explored, and always she made connections and associations. She questioned before she accepted.

> I have given a different interpretation to Elvas' 'six days.' (p. 166). Observe that he says, 'They passed through a province called Catalte; and, (isn't this 'and' equivalent to 'then'?) going through a desert six days' journey in extent. . .' Doesn't he mean that they had *already* passed through Catalte (we don't know *how* big), and the six days was taken up passing through the deserted country, only?[22]

When she made any discovery, she eagerly shared it. In November of 1936 she learned that Captain George Prince, an old steamboat captain from Natchez, had personally seen two mounds that she and Swanton had been trying to place. She prefaced the news to Swanton with "I am scorching the typewriter ribbon to tell you my news."[23] Swanton too was quick to share findings, maps, and other documents with Dormon.

Ultimately the committee members assembled a manuscript of five hundred typewritten pages with several related maps. The De Soto Commission sent to the United State Congress a "satisfactory determination the route of De Soto and his successor Luis de Moscoso, through the southern section of the United States in 1539-1543."[24] The commission had undertaken the task of unraveling controversies that surrounded De Soto's expedition. The table of contents for the manuscript sent to Congress indicates the breadth of historical, ethnological, archaeological, geological, and geographical information researched by the commission. The Smithsonian printed the document.

The commission also requested that Congress validate the De Soto research by funding appropriate celebrations commemorating the quartercentenary of De Soto's expedition. Even before the formal request, Carrie wrote to two congressmen, John H. Overton and Leonard Allen, to enlist their support.

> It has been definitely decided that De Soto did pass through Louisiana, and that he did die in what is now this state, on the

> banks of the Mississippi River. (You know this has been a disputed question among historians.) In view of these facts, know you will be interested in seeing that Louisiana has her full share in the proposed quadricentennial celebration.[25]

The commission asked for a five-million-dollar appropriation; they received one hundred thousand dollars designated for participation in a Pan-American Fair at Tampa, Florida. The Florida Fair Association invited Dormon to be one of the honorary sponsors of the Pan American-De Soto Exposition. Carrie accepted. Her acceptance, though, was more than honorific. She wrote the Fair Association, offering suggestions about Indian and Spanish costumes as well as about permanent exhibits.[26]

In 1939 Swanton encouraged Dormon to write her own account of the De Soto expedition:

> It seems to me that during the next twelve months the market should be ripe for a popular and simple, but romantically couched, narrative of De Soto's career. There is positively no good one that is up to date. That by Theodore Maynard has a number of wretched blunders and it is out of print anyhow. After all that has happened, I don't want you to sidetrack for anything tangible and immediate for an uncertain flyer, but if there is any kind of market for such a work—and I am sure there is—one coming from a member of the De Soto Commission should have a sale. This is by way of suggestion.[27]

Dormon did work on such a book but never published her story. Nevertheless, Dormon had served and served well on the De Soto Commission.

Notes

1. "Report of the United States De Soto Expedition Commission," Public Resolution No. 57, 74th United States Congress, August 26, 1935, Caroline Dormon Collection, Cammie G. Henry Research Center, Watson Memorial Library, Northwestern State University, Natchitoches, Louisiana, Folder 1386

2. *Ibid.*

3. Notes and letters, Folder 1229.

4. Dr. John R. Swanton, Smithsonian Institute, letter to Caroline Dormon, September 19, 1932, Folder 1365.

5. "Report of the United States De Soto Expedition Commission," Public Resolution No. 57, 74th United States Congress, August 26, 1935, Folder 1386.

6. Caroline Dormon, letter to Dr. John R. Swanton, January 26, 1936, Folder 1370.

7. *Ibid.*

8. *Ibid.*

9. Letters, Folder 1372.

10. Dr. John R. swanton, letter to Caroline Dormon, May 29, 1936, Folder 1372.

11. Caroline Dormon, letter to Col. John R. Fordyce, June 5, 1936, Folder 1408.

12. Caroline Dormon, letter to Col. John R. Fordyce, September 23, 1936, Folder 1409.

13. "Report of the United States De Soto Expedition Commission," Public Resolution No. 57, 74th United States Congress, August 26, 1935, Folder 1386.

14. Notes, Folder 1387.

15. Caroline Dormon, story related by Richard Johnson.

16. Caroline Dormon, letter to Mr. Geddes, United States Engineer's Office, Natchez, Mississippi, September 14, 1936, Folder 1422.

17. Caroline Dormon, letter to Dr. John R. Swanton.

18. Caroline Dormon, letter to Dr. John R. Swanton, October 13, 1936, Folder 1374.

19. Dr. John R. Swanton, letter to Caroline Dormon, October 20, 1936, Folder 1374.

20. Caroline Dormon, letter to Dr. John R. Swanton, October 26, 1936, Folder 1374.

21. Caroline Dormon, letter to Dr. John R. Swanton, October 25, 1936, Folder 1374.

22. Caroline Dormon, letter to Dr. John R. Swanton, October 26, 1936, Folder 1374.

23. Caroline Dormon, letter to Dr. John R. Swanton, November 2, 1936, Folder 1374.

24. "Report of the United States De Soto Expedition Commission," Public Resolution No. 57, 74th United States Congress, August 26, 1935, Folder 1386.

25. Caroline Dormon, letter to Sen. John H. Overton, January 5, 1937, Folder 1426.

26. Notes and letters, Folders 1414 and 1376.

27. Dr. John R. Swanton, letter to Caroline Dormon, March 11, 1939, Folder 1379.

LANDSCAPING WITH NATURE

Dormon defined landscaping in terms of nature:

> Perfect landscaping is doing the work in such an artfully-natural manner that it appears as if no planting has been done. The finished product closely approximates Nature at her best. Nowhere is this so true as in the landscaping of roadsides. These are most beautiful when they simply become a part of the surrounding countryside.[1]

Because of this perspective and her knowledge of native trees and plants, Carrie was charged with the responsibility of landscaping the forty acres of ground at the Midstate Hospital in Pineville.[2] In February 1938, A. R. Johnson, director of the Department of Public Welfare; Ed Neild, Shreveport architect for the hospital; and U. B. Evans, chair of the Advisory Board of the hospital recommended that Dormon be hired to plan and direct the planting of a Louisiana garden. Such a garden would afford a pleasant woodland setting for patients as well as showcase indigenous flora of the state. This was the demonstration for which Carrie had campaigned. Of the appointment Dormon remarked: "For twenty years I have been writing articles and giving lectures extolling native planting, and now I have had my hand called." In a letter to A. R. Johnson, she elaborated: "I have long wanted to show the world just what Louisiana has in the way of native flora." She signed the letter "Yours for Louisiana."[3]

The grounds at the hospital had formerly been the site of the Labat house, which had been abandoned for more than fifty years. Carrie wanted to keep the graceful hills and dells of the previous home. She and the workers—primarily from the National Youth Administration—began gingerly clearing brush. From the undergrowth emerged thirty-five different native species, including five kinds of oak, catalpa, swamp privet, silver bell, and the cotton bush.

Once again, Carrie was asked to define her job, for there was no previous job description on which to rely. She decided to categorize the work by actual stages involved in the planting, rather than by time frames or by bedding acreage. She divided the scope of her work into three areas: planning, cooperation, inspection. In the planning stage, Carrie designed a layout, selected the species to be planted, and determined a schedule of planting. This stage also included the arrangement of work to be done month by month, an arrangement that allowed for the variable of weather. Carrie planned for a greenhouse so that cuttings from native plants could be rooted and grown in containers for permanent planting. In the next stage, cooperation, Carrie supervised her assistant, Robert E. Hoke, as well as other workers. She secured plant donations and other materials. Further, she coordinated the equipment for soil additions. The final stage was termed inspection. Carrie inspected the initial clearing of the brush, the selection of the plants themselves, and the actual planting.[4]

Even though Carrie would not receive official notice of her appointment as supervisor of planting for Midstate Charity Hospital grounds until June 7, 1938, by late February 1938, she had sent A. R. Johnson, commissioner of public welfare and acting state hospital director, preliminary pastel drawings of the hospital grounds as they would appear by the spring of 1940. Carrie forwarded monthly summaries of her work. She was allowed a per diem rate of $5.00 per 24 hours even for "exploring" trips, and she was encouraged to accept invitations to speak to clubs and organizations about the hospital landscaping.[5]

Much work had to be done simply to ready the grounds for grass and plants. Carrie wrote A. R. Johnson of progress in July 1939:

> To most people, just the growing of grass sounds very prosaic, but greening up the approach to our hospital has taken on the proportion of an adventure. You see, everyone said we could not make it grow on that clay this time of year. But we have done just that.[6]

The adventure included placing cherry laurels on the two hundred foot wide approach. Carrie knew that such planting would give the "hurrying public something to see from Main Street."[7] She added groupings of hundreds of redbuds, dogwoods, fringe trees, hollies, wild azaleas, magnolias, and wild hydrangeas. She accented the front of the building with semi-formal mass planting of yaupon, dahoon holly, wild sweet olive, and andromeda. In

Courtesy Northwestern State University

Caroline Dormon with Mayor Rollo Lawrence at Midstate Charity Hospital, Pineville, Louisiana.

Caroline Dormon

Courtesy Northwestern State University

other areas she planted sourwood, tulip trees, crabapples, winter willow, sloe, and cherokee rose. She also planned a cutting garden so that some flowers could be brought inside the hospital.[8]

What was not an adventure was again dealing with politics. When Robert Hoke was hired as Carrie's assistant, a man named Stokes protested that he had not been hired. He dissented so loudly that Carrie even spoke to his father to secure help in stopping his "clanging tongue."[9] Stokes was eventually sent to Carrie as a caretaker, and he continued to cause dissension. He absented himself from work without informing anyone, he left work undone, and, according to Carrie, his tongue "never ceases."[10] He had been hired as a caretaker although the grounds were not finished.

In fact, by July 1940 Carrie became increasingly more concerned about budget cutbacks. She estimated that the grounds could be completed in two months at a modest cost:

plants and fertilizer	$ 111.00
salary for Hoke (2 months)	250.00
salary for Dormon (2 months)	400.00
common labor	320.00
expenses, incidentals	100.00
	$1181.00[11]

J. E. Snee, director of the Department of Institutions, however, wrote Carrie that he could not find this amount of money in the hospital budget or in the administrative budget. Carrie requested that at least her assistant, Hoke, be retained through the rest of the summer months so that he could water the plants and check the weeds and grass. Snee had initmated that by October Carrie would be rehired to finish the planting, the money being dependent on the political situation. Still on leave in November, Carrie appealed to Snee:

> I had hoped to hear from you before this, offering some definite plans for the completion of the hospital grounds. You have, on several occasions, expressed your eagerness to see the work finished. I was delighted when you said that we could have a truck at Pineville and that you would give us several good hands

> (laborers). If you could have done this, and let me resume my work the first of November (as I expected), the planting at Pineville would have been nearing completion at this time. . . .
>
> I have put every particle of brain and talent I possessed into this project—creating a distinctive type of planting of public grounds in Louisiana. And I was sure of its appeal to those who handled the finances of the state because it was so much more economical than the plan followed heretofore. It must be remembered that I was doing this at a time when the state was pouring out untold thousands of dollars on landscaping public grounds and planting highways. . . .
>
> Then, just as I thought my troubles were over, came the various changes in state organization. When the reorganization first began, I realized that my work would have to held in suspension for a while. . . .
>
> Now the 'leave' has lengthened into almost four months, during which time I have gone right along directing the work and making a number of trips at my own expense. I did this voluntarily because I know the value of this work to the state, and I could not bear to see it lost. . . .[12]

Carrie had to battle budget funds and politics as well as the corollary newcomers of political change. The men who had appointed Carrie to the project were no longer in control. With the project only two months from completion, Carrie was unable to convince Snee to allow her to complete the grounds. In a letter to Edgar B. Stern of New Orleans, Carrie summarized her frustration about ever-changing politics and her fear about the disintegration of her work on the hospital grounds:

> When Mr. Henican was appointed, I was faced with the problem of trying to acquaint him with the very complicated program I had undertaken in this hospital planting. There is no doubt that he came into the office prejudiced against everything in the previous organization. This made it even more difficult for me. No matter what anyone may say against A. R. Johnson, he was a man of vision, and a fair and just person. *He* knew my family and

> what they had always stood for. He knew that I had a fine job, and an established reputation in my line of work before the Long Regime came in. And he knew that I resigned my position (I was getting 200 dollars per month, and expenses with the Dept. of Conservation, which was very good salary for a woman at that time) when Huey Long was first elected Governor. Although Mr. Johnson knew that my whole family had always fought the Longs bitterly, he gave me this position, and gave me his *loyal support* when I was heckled by the Long adherents in Alexandria. . . . Mr. Johnson did this work for three reasons: first, he knew it was a real economy program; second, he sincerely admired our native trees and flowers, and wanted to see them used for the public planting; and, last, he felt that it was simple justice to give me this opportunity to show the public the value of my work. But, how, I pray, could I make our present political leaders believe this?. . . then came Mr. Snee. . . . He even intimated that he was going to turn our beautiful grounds over to a landscape man. . . . I could visualize exactly what would happen. Our beautiful native evergreens—star anise, andromeda, dahoon holly, mountain laurel (filled with bloom buds), gordonia, etc.—would be torn out and masses of arbor vitae and ligustrums substituted. Our lovely restful open spaces, rolling hills and hollows, softly carpeted with green, would be cut up into formal horrors—crescents, stars, and diamonds—and filled with petunias, salvias, and periwinkles. (He did mention the word 'beds,' and I shivered.)"[13]

Realizing the immovable barriers, Carrie wrote Snee November 30, 1940:

> First, though, to keep the issue from becoming clouded: I no longer desire to be employed by the Dept. of Institutions, in any capacity whatever. So what I now say you will understand is entirely selfless, with no personal motive behind it. . . . I was most surprised by your vehement objection to the mild cost of completing the planting, as it was *you* who wanted to hire more help, and even buy a few shrubs, to hasten the completion of the

project. As this fell right in with my wishes in the matter, I agreed, and, at your request, got up figures for your consideration.

It had not been my plan to buy anything more, but to continue getting plants from the woods. As I told you, of course, we would have to have the use of a truck for part of the time in order to carry the program out in that way.

You were the one who seemed dissatisfied with the grounds (at our first conference). I think they are lovely just as they stand, and will be fairly well satisfied with results, if we can only finish setting the shrubs from the slathouse and the reserve garden.[14]

Finally, she entreated Snee to maintain the native plantings by hiring someone with horticultural training. Carrie had not been allowed to complete the grounds as she had planned, but she could be well satisfied with her accomplishments. She had arranged primarily donated plants into a beautiful native garden for public grounds.

Notes

1. Caroline Dormon, typed circular titled "Roadside Beauty in Louisiana," Caroline Dormon Collection, Cammie G. Henry Research Center, Watson Memorial Library, Northwestern State University, Natchitoches, Louisiana, Folder 1196.

2. A. R. Johnson, State Hospital Director, letter to Caroline Dormon, June 7, 1938, Folder 634.

3. Caroline Dormon, letter to A. R. Johnson, February 16, 1938, Folder 634.

4. Caroline Dormon, typed notes titled "Planting State Charity Hospital Grounds," Folder 1179.

5. A. R. Johnson, letter to Caroline Dormon, March 16, 1938, Folder 634.

6. Caroline Dormon, letter to A. R. Johnson, July 12, 1939, Folder 635.

7. Caroline Dormon, letter to A. R. Johnson, November 16, 1939, Folder 635.

8. Caroline Dormon, letter to A. R. Johnson, September 25, 1939, Folder 639.

9. Caroline Dormon, letter to A. R. Johnson, October 13, 1939, Folder 639.

10. *Ibid.*

11. Caroline Dormon, quoted by J. E. Snee, Director, Department of Institutions, letter to Caroline Dormon, November 27, 1940, Folder 1191.

12. Caroline Dormon, letter to J. E. Snee, Director, Department of Institutions, November 22, 1940, Folder 1191.

13. Caroline Dormon, letter to Edgar B. Stern, New Orleans, December 4, 1940, Folder 1202.

14. Caroline Dormon, letter to J. E. Snee, November 30, 1940, Folder 1191.

"HIGHWAYS PLUS TREES"

The first article Dormon published, "Highways Plus Trees" *in Holland's Magazine*, had been about highway beauty. Carrie had seen the beauty of Southern highways, but she knew it was not the result of intentionality:

> . . . It is a sort of accidental beauty, most of our trees being merely relics and remnants of the magnificent forests with which we of the South were so richly endowed. Rarely now one may pass through a tract of virgin timber, but even where the merchantable timber has been cut away, attractive trees are left which—where fires have not taken their bitter toll—add charm to the road.[1]

Roadside improvement continued to concern Carrie. She had traveled over the state, had studied highway conditions, had taken photographs, had written articles, had delivered lectures, had "lived it."[2] From these experiences she noted four major concerns. First, she emphasized the necessity of preservation and conservation, saving the trees and shrubs that were already growing along highways as well as keeping the areas clean. Second, she suggested that when additional plants were needed that the plants should be chosen "to dazzle visitors with sheets of our colorful Louisiana."[3] Third, she addressed the issue of erosion, stressing the use of spreading plants to hold the soil. Fourth, she sought cooperation among clubs, state services, federal agencies, and private landowners. In December, 1940, Carrie sent these objectives to Prescott Foster, director of Louisiana Department of Highways. Foster not only agreed with Carrie's plan, but he also asked her to direct the plan. She would work directly under Foster.

Again, Carrie was a pioneer. There was not even a job title for this new position. Although garden club advisor and roadside improvement advisor were suggested, Foster and Harry Henderlite, chief engineer for the Highway Department, decided upon highway beautification consultant. Carrie bantered: "My title sounds a little top-heavy!"[4] In response to a request to speak, Carrie pleaded: "What a title! I hope it doesn't prejudice you!"[5] Then the Department of Civil Service sent Carrie employment forms with her title listed as "beautician." In a letter to the Department of

Civil Service, Carrie asked that a correction be made, explaining "My work is quite different."[6]

The title, however, was not the only bureaucratic hurdle. Carrie was given report sheets that were typically used by employees engaged in construction. The report asked for hours and minutes, dollars and cents, items that could be charted in blocks.[7] Carrie's work was too various to be reported in such a blank, for a single day often involved sixteen hours of work.

Carrie was excited about this position, but she was also circumspect. The state was in a period of re-organization. Even before the announcement of her position, she wrote Foster about premature publicity.

> Planned publicity is a wonderful force, but T. N. T. has to be handled with care and knowledge. No one knows better than I that everything connected with state affairs must be approached cautiously as this time. My intention was this: to work out a systematic, coordinated, informed publicity program, then go over it carefully with you and Mr. Henderlite before launching the same.[8]

After the announcement, Carrie began work. She penned resolutions, asking the Highway Department to commit itself to preserving shrubs and trees along the highways, asking the U. S. Forest Service to run double fire lanes to protect trees, asking police juries to forbid dumping on their respective parish roads. Carrie wrote to other states to secure information about their conservation programs and about their tourist income. She obtained copies of laws which protected wildflowers and other native plants. Carrie summarized the early progress: "Even *I*—after hammering at this thing for twenty years—am surprised at the way it is sweeping along."[9] Carrie explained the positive response to the beautification plan with a comparison:

> The first time I ever planted an acorn, I got impatient because nothing appeared above the surface as quickly as I wanted, so I dug it up to see what had happened. Lo, it had a fine root several inches long![10]

Carrie felt that this story paralleled the conservation work in Louisiana. The previous years of work by so many had not produced much above the surface, but the roots had continued to grow.

Specific groups requested Carrie's advice. The Shreveport Beautification Foundation, a division of the Shreveport Chamber of Commerce, enlisted her services in making long range plans for the city. Carrie first suggested that the foundation concentrate on particular projects rather than scattering its efforts. One such project was the drive around Cross Lake. Carrie surveyed the area, finding minimal planting necessary:

> But the thing that impressed me the most of all is that Nature has massed all sorts of beautiful flowering shrubs and trees along the Drive, for almost its entire length. Why, *planting* is needed in a few places, only. If you can save the dogwood, wild plum, hawthorne (several kinds), and redbuds (yes, *redbuds—great* masses of them, growing in every hollow!), the reputation of this drive will go abroad in the land.[11]

Next, Carrie researched zoning laws to determine the legal restrictions that could be placed on businesses as well as the prohibitions against billboards. The foundation planted 10,000 redbuds as its first official project. Carrie was invited to deliver an illustrated lecture at the celebration ceremony.[12]

Carrie also selected the plants for Cross Lake Hatchery. The *Shreveport Times* reported that the fish were "swishing their tails in applause"[13] for Miss Caroline Dormon. For the landscaping, Carrie primarily used native plants, relying on only one cultivated plant for color, crepe myrtles. Another foundation project with which Carrie helped was Fort Humbug. Carrie found the grounds at the fort outstanding: "The rare Chinquapin oak, Quercua Muhlenberrgil, is a beautiful tree, and there are several fine specimens there. I, myself, have found it *nowhere else* in Louisiana."[14] Carrie urged the foundation members to consider preservation as a priority in landscaping the Fort.

Other requests came from a variety of clubs, including men's clubs. Carrie found that men were especially interested. She reasoned: "Making our highways beautiful is now a business proposition, so the men *ought* to be interested."[15]

Although Carrie was inundated with requests for articles, speeches, and advice, she wished to include all groups with a shared interest. She wrote Clara L. Knott, Many, Louisiana, who had been appointed chair of roadside beautification for the Federation of Women's Clubs: "I have had more invitations than I could fill, from Chambers of Commerce, Garden Clubs, men's business clubs, etc. The project is going strong—but it is certainly not complete without the Federation in the van."[16] Undaunted by their initial silence, Carrie continued writing to individual clubs offering to make talks and distributing plans for roadside planting. Soon the clubs were scheduling her for programs and adopting her plans. In fact, Ida M. Chapman, chair of roadside beautification for Covington Garden Club, wrote that Carrie's plans could "not be improved upon."[17]

As part of her original improvement plan, Carrie entreated the Highway Department to interject itself into more judicious clearing along roads. Carrie felt that the problem stemmed from untrained workers and supervisors who ruined living trees by burning brush on rights-of-way. She felt that these workers did not appreciate the difference between "brush" and "bushes." Like other issues Carrie championed, this issue involved no additional expense and actually effected savings. Trees and shrubs were being burned and then had to be replaced at a cost to taxpayers. Carrie had first written the Highway Department about the unrestrained burnings and cuttings in August of 1941. Six months later she was still writing, reporting burnings of "extra vigor" and cuttings of yaupons which "would sell for ten dollars each." Carrie pointed out specific areas where the burnings and cuttings occurred.[18]

Carrie had traveled widely throughout the state to identify particularly attractive drives. She lobbied to see that these areas remained naturally beautiful. Among the areas she so designated were roads between Bogalusa and Franklinton; Amite and Baton Rouge; Greenwood and Texas line; Jena, Harrisonburg, and Sicily Island; Monroe and Columbia; Baton Rouge and Gonzales; Shreveport and Vivian. She recommended that maintenance crews be instructed to leave these areas untouched. They had attractive low shrubs and flowers, including winter willow, wax myrtle, daubentonia, and red maple. She appealed to Harry Henderlite, chief engineer for the Department of Highways:

> The more I think it over, the more I am convinced that you do not understand what I am talking about in regard to roadsides. You know all about fills and grades and slopes and elevations—and all the other mysterious things which engineers are so familiar with—but you *don't* know what is happening to the landscape through which your roads pass. You sit in your office and plan the intricate network of highways over the state, but you don't know what happens sometimes when the plan is slapped onto the fair earth. . . .
>
> It will do little good for an engineer who has little or no authority to go out with me and look at it—he will just repeat mass orders very glibly—and where will we be? Just where we started. No, the orders will have to stem from the *top*. So I DARE you to go out with the engineer and me (on Tuesday or Wednesday), drive from Baton Rouge to Bogalusa, and see for yourself. I believe that you will realize that I am not talking of something unreasonable or impossible. It is more a question of leaving the roadside *alone* than doing *more*. . . .
>
> Please get this thought clearly: instead of asking the Department to spend more money, I am beseeching that you spend far *less*.[19]

Carrie reminded Henderlite of his fondness for red maples and explained that road crews were clearing the roadsides of maples and indiscriminately leaving other trees. Again, she was asking to save, not to spend.

Another highway issue was roadside litter. Unless dumping were stopped, few travelers would notice any roadside trees or shrubs. At Carrie's urging, Foster had signs made that prohibited dumping on rights-of-way at a penalty of one hundred dollars.[20] Despite the signs, Carrie noticed that dumping continued. Even businesses littered. Carrie asked Foster for permission to speak to offenders. She bargained: "Of course, I will be polite about it the *first* time I warn them!"[21] She also enlisted the help of the Garden Club Federation in shaping public opinion to support the law.

Besides the actual roadsides, Carrie wished to see all areas of the state beautified. She wrote Lt. Col. John A. Smith, Jr., Camp Polk: "I have been much disturbed over the desert-like appearance of the various army camps in our State."[22] She offered to help plan the grounds. She knew the camp had special needs, plants that would help the sandy soil, that would grow quickly, that would require low maintenance. Carrie wished to intervene before the camp bought "catalog" plants that would not thrive in Louisiana's extreme weather. This fear was real. "After having seen arbor vitae planted around CCC camps, nothing would surprise me."[23] Carrie knew that the war itself had made necessary the cutting of thousands of trees for army camps, and she wanted to compensate by re-planting, especially since the camps now had unlimited labor. She also wished to beautify the soldiers' quarters which she found "so bleak that they [must] feel as if they (the soldiers) are in the guardhouse."[24]

Carrie's work was not limited to speaking and advising. She had many other plans in mind. She proposed a state nursery that would supply the native trees and shrubs to be used along highways, for Carrie knew that the economical plan for highway planting would require thousands of native plants. In a state nursery, cuttings could be made and plants could be grown from seed. Plants supplied in these ways would certainly be economical. The nursery would differ from the forestry nursery which limited production to commercial species. She envisioned a minimal investment since the state had land and one horticulturist could oversee the project.[25]

Part of Carrie's work consisted of censure. Some conservation leaders in the state, including leaders of the Louisiana Federation of Women's Clubs, presented plans for a legislative resolution that would ask the Highway Department to fence all the highways in the state. "The idea of the Highway Department fencing 38,000 miles of highway staggers the imagination. And the maintenance of same would be stupendous."[26] Carrie further rebutted that it would be more economical to pass state stock laws.

Another occasion demanded objection. The Department of Conservation decided to re-issue the Arbor Day program Carrie had devised, but the department had added a note that teachers should secure trees for planting from roadsides. Carrie was concerned that this "thoughtless" advice would have damaging effects not only in the senseless digging of trees but also in the model to children that such digging was proper. Carrie asked M.

E. Brashears, forester in the Department of Conservation, to have the note about digging omitted. Brashears countered that teachers could remove trees that would "in the course of time" be destroyed. Carrie knew that few teachers or any others could accurately determine which plants "in the course of time" would be destroyed.[27] Carrie then requested John Coxe, state superintendent of education, to include a letter to teachers instructing them to disregard the sentence about digging on roadsides. She reminded Coxe that it was against the law to dig on rights-of-way.[28]

Carrie's tenure as highway beautification consultant was filled with additional campaigns. She lobbied to limit the number of billboards on the highways, but some legislators owned outdoor advertising companies. She lobbied for legislation to prohibit utility companies from leaving trimmed brush from lines where it fell, but some state officials owned stock in utility companies.

Carrie had to battle lack of concern, commitment, and organization in addition to state budgets and politics. As a result, on January 15, 1943, Carrie tendered her resignation to Prescott Foster, still pleading for roadside improvement.

> You will recall that I told you the other day of my plan to resign, effective the last of this month.
>
> You have been fine, and it has been a pleasure to work with you. Naturally, I will still be interested in preserving and enhancing the beauty of our roadsides, as I have always been for many years past. I know that keeping roadsides attractive has an actual cash value beyond estimating and that by preserving as much *natural* beauty as is possible, the state will be saved many thousands of dollars. Also, keeping a mat of vines and other low growth on backslopes cuts maintenance costs in half.
>
> You have copies of my plans, and when I can help to make them clearer or assist in any way toward their execution, please call on me. If these plans are carried out as work progresses, the roadside can be made and kept attractive at almost *no cost.*
>
> With all good wishes.[29]

Notes

1. Caroline Dormon, "Highways Plus Trees," Holland's Magazine, April 1923, Caroline Dormon Collection, Cammie G. Henry Research Center, Watson Memorial Library, Northwestern State University, Natchitoches, Louisiana, Folder 776.

2. Caroline Dormon, letter to Mary Land Lock, Department of Conservation, December f26, 1940, Folder 1215.

3. Caroline Dormon, letter to W. Prescott Foster, Director of Louisiana Department of Highways, December 11, 1940, Folder 1201.

4. Caroline Dormon, letter to W. H. Hodges, Jr., January 29, 1941, Folder 1206.

5. Caroline Dormon, letter to Mrs. Moritz, June 3, 1941, Folder 1217.

6. Caroline Dormon, letter to Department of State Civil Service, May 7, 1942, Folder 1214.

7. Caroline Dormon, letter to Prescott Foster, February 13, 1941, Folder 1207.

8. Caroline Dormon, letter to Prescott Foster, December 27, 1940, Folder 1201.

9. Caroline Dormon, lettter to Mrs. Reily, February 14, 1941, Folder 546.

10. Caroline Dormon, letter to Mr. Ovid N. Butler, Ed., American Forests and Foresty Life, Washington, D. C., March 26, 1941, Folder 1220.

11. Caroline Dormon, letter to L. A. Mailhes, President, Shreveport Beautification Foundation, April 13, 1941, Folder 951.

12. Notes and letters, Folder 957.

13. Shreveport Times, April 16, 1942, Folder 1169.

14. Caroline Dormon, letter to Mrs. Falaitz, January 31, 1943, Folder 957.

15. Caroline Dormon, letter to Mrs. Moritz, June 3, 1941, Folder 1217.

16. Caroline Dormon, Letter to Clara L. Knott, April 8, 1941, Folder 1223.

17. Ida M. Chapman, letter to Caroline Dormon, July 30, 1941, Folder 543.

18. Caroline Dormon, letter to Prescott Foster, February 9, 1942, Folder 1210.

19. Caroline Dormon, letter to Harry B. Henderlite, December 7, 1941, Folder 1206.

20. Notes and letters, Folder 1222.

21. Caroline Dormon, letter to Prescott Foster, October 26, 1942, Folder 1210.

22. Caroline Dormon, letter to Lt. Col. John A. Smith, Jr., August 23, 1941, Folder 1167.

23. Caroline Dormon, letter to Major Val Irion, Camp Beauregard, August 23, 1941, Folder 1167.

24. *Ibid.*

25. Caroline Dormon, letter to M. E. Brashears, State Forester, Department of Conservation, June 4, 1941, Folder 1212.

26. *Ibid.*

27. Caroline Dormon, letter to M. E. Brashears, December 18, 1941, Folder 1208.

28. Caroline Dormon, letter to John Coxe, State Superintendent of Education, December 31, 1941, Folder 1205.

29. Caroline Dormon, letter to Prescott Foster, January 15, 1943, Folder 1216.

NATURE REMEMBERED

Dormon's writing organically grew from her interests in nature. When asked about the origin of her ambition, she replied:

> I simply loved nature, always, and could no more have stopped studying birds, flowers, and trees and drawing pictures of them, than I could have stopped breathing! Would a thirsty man refuse to drink cool water when he saw it? I wasn't ambitious; I was just doing what I loved. And I began writing nature articles for the same reason—I was just so full of it I had to talk about it. I'll never forget the first check I got. I was all torn up over the destruction of beautiful old trees along the roads that were being made into highways. I wrote a little article, called it 'Highways Plus Trees,' sent it with some pictures, to *Holland's*. I was astonished when they sent me a check for *sixteen dollars*! I have never received a check that was half so wonderful.[1]

Love of nature—not love of money—launched Dormon into the world of writing. Her motivation for writing was to share the "wild things" she knew and loved. Additionally, her magazine writing can be divided into two other categories: articles specifically requested by editors or employers who knew Dormon to be knowledgeable about native plants and articles Dormon penned in order to awaken others to conservation and preservation of nature.

"Save, Oh, Save!" is the title of an article that not only describes some of the native beauty of Louisiana but also pleads for protection of that native beauty:

> Blossom-time will soon be here again—and what so lovely as our own Louisiana woods? Alas, however, with flowers, come flower-pickers. Flower-breakers would be more nearly correct, as some thoughtless ones tear down great branches of blooming dogwood and practically destroy entire plants of wild azalea.[2]

She did not understand the "ruthless" uprooting of plants along the roadside, for she considered the roadside an extension of the home's frontyard. Ruthless uprooting was causing another problem: the uprooting was dangerously diminishing the number of vanishing species.

Always Dormon underscored the beauty of natives, her descriptions frequently being lyrical.

> Dogwood whitens the hillsides, while every stream bank and low ground becomes a mass of dainty pink, the wild azalea. Grand-sir-greybeard puts on his fringe, and masses of lovely crab apple sweeten the air, while the ground beneath is clothed in bright blue and lavender violets, wild phlox, and verbena.[3]

Carrie soon had such a compilation of information about flowers, especially native Louisiana flowers, that she began amassing book-length materials. On January 18, 1934, Carrie mailed the manuscript of *Wild Flowers of Louisiana*, her first book, to H. A. Stevenson of Doubleday-Doran Books, Outdoor Books. The literary relationship she had with Doubleday, though, was difficult. In 1932, Ina Weyrauch, a company editor, wrote Dormon that the book was "a thoroughly fine piece of work. . . . There is no question about the quality of the text and its intrinsic interest and value."[4] The company feared that the book would be too expensive to produce and that sales would be slow. When Carrie received this letter, she forwarded the letter to her "running mate," Cammie Henry of Melrose. At the bottom of the letter Carrie added a note: "Oh, yes! *Very fine—so blamed* fine that nobody will publish it!. . . I've got a scrapbook of nice letters from editors—and can't buy gas to get to Melrose."[5] Carrie did not, however, waver in her belief in the book; she knew that the economic situation of the nation was the reason that publishing companies were skeptical of books without some assurance of sales.

There were others, too, who believed in the book because Caroline's knowledge of flowers was well known. One believer was Edith R. Stern of New Orleans; Mrs. Stern agreed to guarantee the sale of 1038 copies of the book at a cost of $5.00 per book, the total guarantee amounting to $5190.00. In return, Stern received all of the original illustrations from the book, sixty-five watercolors and five black and white plates. Stern paid

Dormon a $750.00 royalty on the first thousand copies and provided Dormon with fifty copies of the book for personal use.[6] Dormon dedicated the book to "Edith Rosenwald Stern and the other flower lovers whose generous interest has made its publication possible, this book is gratefully dedicated."[7]

With the underwriting by Stern, Doubleday would have no advertising expense on these first assured sales, but months of negotiations remained. Business was not Carrie's forte, and, as usual, Carrie needed the money then, not later. She thus agreed to Doubleday's proposal; they would pay her no royalty on the first thousand copies, and fifteen per cent on the following five hundred copies. The book would be listed in trade at a cost of $7.50. There were still delays and disagreements over the number of trade books to be sold, length of time Dormon would have to sell the first thousand copies, postage charges, and the critical issue of shipping dates.[8]

In subsequent correspondence with Dormon, Doubleday made numerous editorial suggestions. For example, H. A. Stevenson asked her to re-color one of the paintings. She, not obliquely, responded:

> Now, I can strengthen outlines, but if the color is deepened or changed, it will just be another glaring misrepresentation of a wild-flower—the very thing I most abhor. The beauty of the water-hyacinth is its delicacy of color. Rather than give it the wrong color, I had rather omit it entirely.[9]

Carrie simply would not allow the integrity of the book to be compromised. The completed manuscript contained 350 native species, with 63 color illustrations and 46 black and white ones. Introductory material included remonstrations directed to plant protection. Carrie listed plants that should "NEVER" be picked or dug, such as wild orchids, Indian pipes, Closed Gentian, Celestials, Eustylis, Herbertia, and Cardinal Flower; plants that should be "PICKED SPARINGLY," such as wild azalea, crabapple, wild phlox, and verbena; and plants that could be enjoyed "FREELY," such as goldenrod, asters, coneflowers, and spider lilies.[10]

This intentional integrity was noticed, for Dormon received extremely favorable reviews from many different sources. An editor from *Better Homes and Gardens* called the book a "splendid piece of work . . . . a job well done."[11] Ethel Hutson, reveiwing for *Home Gardening* wrote: "Looking through the book is like wandering in the woods with a well-posted flower lover who can point out all the shy, rare plans and name the common weeds. . . ."[12] Edgar T. Wherry, eminent botanist affiliated with the University of Pennsylvania, praised the book for "excellent line drawings," "exquisite colored figures," and "helpful notes."[13] F. F. Rockwell, reviewer for the *New York Times*, began his review: "Caroline Dormon has the good fortune to be an artist as well as a tireless student of nature."[14]

In spite of these and numerous other reviews as well as public delight from those who purchased the book, Carrie did not profit financially from the book. She had worked for seven years on the compilation, and she had spent more than a year in the mechanics with Doubleday. In 1935 in a letter to the company, she wrote: "Of course, I showed feeble judgement in ever signing any such unheard of agreement, [but] I intend to fulfill my contract."[15] Doubleday sent small royalty checks for the next several years; often the check for a six month period would be less than twenty dollars. Finally in 1945, Doubleday declared the book out of print and sold Dormon the plates and rights for $250.00.

Plagued by continued financial problems and chronic ill health, Dormon was, nonetheless, undaunted. By 1941, she was already at work on her next book, *Flowers Native to the Deep South*, for she had continued to collect specimens, correspond with botanists, paint species, and observe natives grow. This personal acquaintance with flowers was the essence of Dormon's contribution. She had never purported to be a professional botanist, but she knew that *Magnolia glauca* was easily transplanted while *Magnolia macrophylla* was not. She wished to write a book on native gardening, not a botany. Carrie planned to build on her book, adding new information and drawings. The second book would contain over one hundred figures illustrating flowers found in the Deep South. In fact, Carrie included two species that had never before been listed in any other book. Southern Indian Pipes and Spiranthes odorator had previously been described only in journals. The blurb of the book suggests its scope:

> Fascinating Pitcher-plants, which catch and 'digest' insects; fabulous Louisiana Irises, representing every color in the spectrum;

> exquisite Texas Bluebells—these are but a few of the native plants illustrated and described in this volume.[16]

The book also includes a section of "Flower Tips," with definitions and figures to explain some of the botanical terms. For example, Dormon defines, and thus differentiates, pedicel from petiole. Her careful drawings shows the reader the difference between an oblanceolate leaf and a lanceolate leaf. In the text of the book, Dormon provides information ranging from descriptions for indentifications to growing suggestions for native plants to historical or folk heritage of various species. The entry for Spiderwort family (Commelinaceae—Tradescantia) is representative of this range:

> Seeds of these lovely flowers were sent from America to Tradescant, the gardener of Charles I of England. He grew them successfully, they were immediately popular, and were named in his honor. Then they came back to America, to make their debut as garden flowers! They all have fleshy stems and rather fleshy, blade-like leaves, usually folded one into the other at the base. Each stem bears a cluster of nodding buds and erect, three-petaled flowers. The fragile petals shrivel to a lump of jelly by noon, except on cloudy days.[17]

As Dormon continues to delineate the spiderwort family, the information becomes more specific.

> Western Spiderwort: Tradescantia bracteata
>
> The peculiarity of this species is that the two long bracts supporting the flower cluster are very broad and overlapping. The smooth leaves are distinctly folded and often purplish underneath. Flowers are about 1 1/2 inches in diameter, with broadly ovate, overlapping petals. In color they range from pale blue to violet, and from delicate pink to rose-red, with an occasional one of pure white. With its spidery mass of fleshy roots, it takes transplanting and is most attractive in wild gardens, along drives, etc. It prefers a rather heavy rich soil but will grow almost anywhere. It is found

> in Texas and Louisiana but not east of the Mississippi river (See color plate V.)[18]

Having written the text, Dormon once again began searching for a publisher, and once again she received praise in each rejection slip. More than a decade would pass before a publisher would be found, and, also similar to her first publication experience, this publishing experience was fraught with misunderstandings and difficulties of contracting and financing. Several people offered help to Carrie in the publication of the book. In particular, members of the Louisiana Federated Garden Club proposed financial backing. Jo Evans, chair of the Book Committee of the Louisiana Federated Garden Club, approached Lutcher Stark, a Texas businessman. According to the letter from Evans to Stark, Carrie would sell the manuscript of her book, the new color drawings, the new black and whites, and fifty books for $5000.00, an amount which would be used to begin publication. This was not Carrie's offer. In a letter written to P. M. Parthemore, vice-president of J. Horace McFarland Company, and marked "personal," Carrie explained that the offer was altered without her knowledge and that, consequently, the publication would be delayed.

> A few days ago, Mrs. Gladney [Sarah], President of the La. Garden Club Fed., drove me over into Texas to get certain flowers I wanted for the book. On the trip, she mentioned that Lutcher Stark was to get the metal plates also! I was shocked numb. As soon as I got home, I wrote Mrs. Evans, telling her this, and saying I was sure Mrs. Gladney was mistaken, and please to clear it up. She called me on the phone, and revealed that she had told Mr. Stark on the phone that he could have the plates.[19]

Carrie closed the letter with a note that she was "spiritually and physically" tired. Carrie herself phoned Stark to explain that the plates were not a part of the original $5000.00 offer, for McFarland was charging $4196.00 for the metal plates with their four colors. In addition to the actual cost of the plates, Stark and others considered them collectibles. What followed this unauthorized offer was a series of letters that are not altogether congenial. Evans argued that the plates were not worth anything and that Carrie should not be concerned about them. In fact, Evans wrote Sara Gladney that no one "in the entire South would even store these plates even if she [Dormon] gave them away."[20]

Although Carrie was hurt by such "hard and unsympathetic attitude," there was balance. Edgar Anderson, nationally known botanist, offered to write the blurb for the book; Dr. George Lawrence from the Bailey Hortorium at Cornell University offered to proof the botanical information for the book. With such botanical encouragement, Carrie now needed only financial backing. She turned to A. R. Johnson, a New Orleans banker and friend. Carrie asked Johnson for a loan, hoping to secure the money on the merits of the book itself, for she had no assets to mortgage. Carrie even had "to lay [the manuscript] down now and then to paint an oil picture to sell to buy my daily loaf."[21]

The bank agreed to lend Carrie $7500.00, the garden club guaranteed subscriptions by lending $1200, and four friends—Dorothy Milling, Gladys Reily, Edith Stern, and Jeanne Henderson—made personal loans of $1000.00 each.[22] Carrie called these women "angels." (When the loans to the angels were repaid, all angels except Henderson returned their money to Dormon.) By August 1957, Carrie instructed Parthemore to begin work. Yet misunderstandings and difficulties continued. A. R. Johnson turned the bank loan over to his son who now wanted a mortgage on Briarwood as collateral. Some garden club members themselves wanted to handle the subscriptions. Finally an agreement was reached with Claitor's Book Store, a publishing agent and distributor. Claitor's was to handle all funds from loans or donations as well as sales. A commission or discount of $1.50 on each $7.50 book was given to garden club or book trade sales. According to the agreement, Carrie would receive a fifteen per cent royalty after the publisher, printer, and bank had been repaid.[23]

These agreements made, Carrie began making final corrective changes in the text and in the line drawings. There were delays because of interruptions from visitors. Carrie and her refuge Briarwood had always been sought out. Carrie had now lost her dear sister who shielded her from "every knock on the door, every car toot." Further delays were occasioned by the publishing company. Initially, Parthemore had suggested that a dummy would not have to be made; by September the press had decided that one would be necessary. Carrie still hoped that the book would be available by Christmas. Parthemore wrote her not to worry. Carrie replied: "You send me the recipe for how NOT to worry!"[24] Instead of a recipe Parthemore sent her notice that the book could not be published in less than three months or approximately December 15, 1957. Exasperated, Carrie wrote Frank Gladney, Sara's husband who was a lawyer:

> Do you think it might help for you to write a gentle protest to Mr. Parthemore? Not tough, of course—more of a plea. . . . As long as we have had our agreement, SURELY this work has priority over some of their other orders. . . . This book has truly been my *bete noir*! Never another book for me.[25]

Letters did not effect a Christmas publication date. Carrie next pleaded for March 1958, the date of the state library convention. She began to label the text the "everlasting book," "one of those endless things." McFarland matter-of-factly wired Claitor's: "Impossible to have books by March 27. Letter follows."[26] Bob Claitor forwarded the wire to Carrie with a note that he had not received the follow-up letter. In her return letter to Claitor, Carrie wrote:

> Is this a madman—or just a grand rascal?. . . It certainly looks as if the man simply is not honest. And he was so nice at first!. . . I am like my father; although he was a lawyer, he took it for granted that everyone was honest till proved otherwise. . . . I am not only heartsick, it makes my physically ill.[27]

Carrie went to the library convention without a book, but her talk and the plates she exhibited were well received. The not-yet-out book was placed on the approved list for school libraries.[28]

Flowers Native to the Deep South was released in April of 1958 and included 32 exquisite color plates and 102 beautiful line drawings. Like Dormon's first book, this one received important praise. William Lanier Hunt wrote favorably of the book in his garden column. Elizabeth Lawrence described the book in *The Garden Journal of The New York Botanical Garden* as multi-level work that would appeal to many different groups.

> Written for the layman, who, having found a new flower, cannot rest until it is named . . . it will be of equal use to the botanists studying the flora of the Deep South . . . for the gardener it is a book written by a gardener—one of the best . . . for the student of southern wild flowers it is full of information not to be found elsewhere . . . for collectors of beautiful books it is a treasure.[29]

Katherine S. White, writing for *The New Yorker*, characterized the author as "a gifted collector and a close observer," whose "comments on the many hundreds of wild flowers she does describe are illuminating."[30]

By 1959, a second edition of *Flowers Native to the Deep South* was issued. It too was published by loans and subscriptions.[31] Copies did not sell as rapidly as anticipated. In part, the interest among those in garden clubs seemed to have moved from growing flowers to arranging them. Carrie's indebtedness to the garden federation was not repaid by the end of 1961. Carrie suffered a heart attack on September 20, 1961, an attack which she felt was caused by worry over the book debt and lack of sales.

Despite the worry and the debt, her priority remained: "I cannot afford to have another [heart attack], for some of my seedling Mumes (from Japan) have buds—for the first time—and I MUST see them bloom. . . . Plant a seed, and there is never time to die!"[32]

Dormon's continued interest in flowers mollified the earlier ultimatum: "never another book for me."[33] Carrie now envisioned a book that would present her "successes and failures," thus saving gardeners "headaches and heartaches." The book would not be, as the first two had been, catalogues of plants for identification and cultivation. Rather, Dormon wished to arrange natives according to actual use in certain garden situations. She planned sections or chapters to address particular gardens such as rock gardens, gardens to attract birds, gardens around ponds, and shady trail gardens. Other chapters would focus on seasonal impact: autumn gardens or winter gardens. Still other chapters would emphasize plant groups: iris gardens or bulb gardens.[34]

In 1962, Carrie began corresponding with John Macrae, editor of Outdoor Books for Harper and Row. She forwarded Macrae a rough copy of her new text. She made a request of Macrae: "The first time you read the book, PLEASE read it just for interest, and not in a critical way!"[35] Macrae, though, almost immediately began sending his criticisms. For example, he wanted Dormon to quote other gardeners less and purport the information herself. Dormon replied: "I will not take the responsibility for saying a plant can be grown unless *I have grown it*. I have established a reputation for being accurate and reliable, and I want to maintain it!" Macrae additionally asked Carrie to broaden the geographic scope. She rebutted: "It fairly well covers the United States, from Oregon to Texas, to New England to Florida. I don't see how I could 'broaden it,' unless I include Central and South America." Carrie objected to the changes that altered meaning: "Where I said 'with good root systems,' you wrote in 'adapted.' I mean with good root systems, which is quite different."[36] Carrie especially objected to the criticism that the book relied too heavily upon Briarwood, for Briarwood had been her testing ground for more than forty years and Briarwood was well known in horticultural circles as such. After two years of similar differences, Carrie wrote Macrae:

> What is the use? I rewrite it, incorporating your suggestions—then you send it back again with just as many *more* suggested changes. . . . Please return the manuscript and drawings.[37]

Recounting the problems with Macrae to Elizabeth Lawrence, Carrie wrote: "With such a dictatorial air, there is usually an inner *uncertainty*."[38]

Because Carrie was unsuccessful with publishing houses like Harper, she turned again to Claitor's. The Baton Rouge firm published *Natives Preferred* in 1965. In the introductory material, Carrie explains the title and the rationality of using native plants in the landscape: beauty and adaptability. However, she also pleads for caution. Carrie wanted others to enjoy the beauty of native plants, but she wanted to protect the vanishing floral heritage.

> If this book should cause gardeners to rush out, dig indiscrimately, and bring in plants from the woods, I shall wish I had not spoken. Some years ago I took Dr. Edgar Wherry

> (University of Pennsylvania) to get pictures of an unusual form of *Phlox divaricata* near Shreveport, Louisiana. When we reached the spot, we had to move a brush-heap to find one clump to photograph. 'Why,' I exclaimed, 'they used to cascade all down that bluff!' 'What became of them?' he asked. I shrugged, 'Diggin' Women.' When asked for an explanation I gave it. When he said he would like to write that up for *Wild Flower*, of which he was Editor, I agreed—on condition he would not mention my name. Some of my best friends are 'Diggin' Women'! It happened I knew who had left this lovely spot denuded of its lavendar carpet.[39]

The reviews of *Natives Preferred* were enthusiastic. Elizabeth Lawrence a prolific garden writer herself and the one to whom Carrie dedicated the volume, evaluated the work:

> *Natives Preferred* is a sort of birds-eye view of the flora of the United States, with gleanings from flower growers in all parts of the country. . . . It is also a portrait of Briarwood, Caroline's hundred acre forest, a tapestry woven in loving detail. . . . Only Caroline could have written *Natives Preferred* and only Caroline could have done the sensitive line drawings to go with the text.[40]

Notes

1. Caroline Dormon, typed notes titled "Inquisition," addressed to Mary Belle McKellar, Caroline Dormon Collection, Cammie G. Henry Research Center, Watson Memorial Library, Northwestern State University, Natchitoches, La., Folder 1030.

2. Caroline Dormon, "Save, Oh Save!" *Home Gardening*, (Winter, 1940-1941).

3. *Ibid.*

4. Ina Weyrauch, letter to Caroline Dormon, February 24, 1932, Melrose Scrapbook #213.

5. Caroline Dormon, handwritten note added to Ina Weyrauch letter, Scrapbook #213.

6. Notes and documents regarding book contract, Folder 1020

7. Caroline Dormon, *Wild Flowers of Louisiana* (New York: Doubleday and Doran, 935).

8. Notes and documents regarding book contract, Folders 1022 and 1023.

9. Caroline Dormon, letter to H. A. Stevenson, July 18, Folder 1023.

10. Caroline Dormon, *Wild Flowers of Louisiana.*

11. Editor, *Better Homes and Garden,* Melrose Scrapbook, 2B.

12. Ethel Hutson, *Home Gardening,* Melrose Scrapbook, 2B.

13. Edgar T. Wherry, Folder 245.

14. F. F. Rockwell, *New York Times,* September 22, 1935, Folder 1027.

15. Caroline Dormon, letter to Doubleday, 1935, Foler 45.

16. Caroline Dormon, *Flowers Native to the Deep Sout*h (Baton Rouge: Claitor's, 1959).

17. Caroline Dormon, *Flowers Native to the Deep South,* pp. 8-9.

18. Caroline Dormon, *Flowers Native to the Deep South,* p. 9.

19. Caroline Dormon, letter to P. M. Parthemore, June 13, 1957, Folder 1260.

20. Jo Evans, letter to Sara Gladney, Briarwood.

21. Caroline Dormon, letter to Camilla Bradley, July 26, 1957, Folder 1273.

22. Notes, Folder 1248.

23. Notes, Folder 1246.

24. Caroline Dormon, letter to P. M. Parthemore, Briarwood.

25. Caroline Dormon, letter to Frank Gladney, September 10, 1957, Folder 1254.

26. McFarland Company, wire to Caroline Dormon, Folder 1247.

27. Caroline Dormon, letter to Bob Claitor, March 8, 1958, Folder 1247.

28. Notes, Folders 1248 and 1264.

29. Elizabeth Lawrence, *The Garden Journal of The New York Botanical Garden,* (November-December 1958), Folder 1269.

30. Katherine S. White, *The New Yorker,* (September 24, 1960), Folder 414.

31. Notes, Folders 1256 and 1266.

32. Caroline Dormon, letter to Mrs. Smith, December 15, 1961, Folder 1253.

33. Caroline Dormon, letter to Frank Gladney, September 10, 1957, Folder 1254.

34. Notes, Folder 1016.

35. Caroline Dormon, letter to John Macrae, March 5, 1961, Folder 1016.

36. Caroline Dormon, letter to John Macrae, July 20, 1964, Folder 1016.

37. Caroline Dormon, letter to John Macrae, June 29, 1964, Folder 1016.

38. Caroline Dormon, letter to Elizabeth Lawrence, Elizabeth Lawrence Collection, #35.

39. Caroline Dormon, *Natives Preferred* (Baton Rouge: Claitor's, 1965), pages viii-ix.

40. Elizabeth Lawrence, *Charlotte Observer*, Folder 1019.

NATURE'S ARTIST

One of the most well-known anecdotes about Caroline Dormon involves her single-mindedness when painting. In "Plantation Memo," December 20, 1971, Francois Mignon related the story as part of his public tribute to Carrie:

> Keen of sight and artistic to the tips of fingers, Carrie, like many great artists, was seemingly indifferent to mundane matters that consume so much substance of most mortals. A case in point was a visit to Melrose one summer's day when Caroline, who had been working in her garden at Briarwood, some forty miles away, accepted the invitation of a passing friend to ride with her down to see Mrs. Cammie Henry in the Cane River Country. It happened that some iris in the Melrose garden had just reached the perfection of their spring flowering, and Carrie decided to remain for a day or two to capture them with paint and brush.
>
> As Mrs. Henry used to laughingly recall to Carrie and other friends on the plantation, 'I never saw anyone so intent on their work as was Carrie on that occasion. Unmindful of food or rainment, she came in to dinner only when summoned, and at night after she gone to bed exhausted, I would gather up her clothes and drop them out the window, below which waited a house servant who laundered them during the night and laid them out fresh and tidy on Carrie's chair before she was up the next morning. Carrie was utterly oblivious to these nocturnal efforts, but after a week had passed,—actually it was eleven days—she remarked 'I simply must go back to Briarwood today and get me some fresh clothes since I haven't changed these during the whole past week.'[1]

Carrie preferred painting natural things although she did not pretend to duplicate nature:

> Moonlight is like snow—it blots out all ugliness and emphasizes the beautiful. I wish I could make a picture of my

Courtesy Northwestern
State University

Caroline Dormon painting at Melrose.

> trees, especially the beeches and the maples, against the night sky. I lie in my bed and study them, but I can't quite decide how Nature does it.[2]

Whenever possible, Carrie painted from the natural plants. "To paint wild flowers they must be studied when they are fresh. They are so delicate that they wilt readily. So I raise them and then draw them."[3] No doubt, Carrie preferred to spend her days tending her flowers rather than painting them, but there were times when she exclaimed: "I am eager to paint—my fingers are just tingling for the brush."[4] The majority of Carrie's paintings were of flowers and shrubs and trees.* Carrie used these paintings to illustrate her articles, books, and lectures. Her representations were a skillful combination of correct botany and colored charm.

Carrie sketched and painted covers for Louisiana Society of Horticultural Research publications, iris bulletins and journals, and state forestry materials.[5] She prepared the Louisiana page for Helen Hull's *Wild Flowers for Your Garden*. She also illustrated Elizabeth Lawrence's *Gardening in Winter*. James R. Harolow, managing editor for the American Horticultural Society, praised Dormon's art work: "How perfect your pen and ink drawings turned out to illustrate your 'Chinese Quince' article for the January issue of *The American Horticultural Magazine*."[6] As early as 1927 *The Ladies' Home Journal* paid $75.00 for five drawings by Carrie. *American Home* also published some of her paintings in 1934.

Carrie received numerous requests for commissioned work. Individuals like William Fitzhugh, Legal Division of Arkansas Fuel Oil Company, and studios like Willard E. Worden of San Francisco requested paintings.[7] Carrie rarely painted "orders." "Truly, if someone orders a specific thing, and describes it exactly, with ironbound requirements, I CANNOT paint a stroke."[8] She did, however, take pleasure in painting for friends.

> Josephine Brian Ducournau wants the cypress-by-the-lake picture, and one of Indian pipes. And A. R. Johnson wants the dogwood-in-longleaf pine. This is sold, but I have already begun

* Carrie painted only a few portraits. Among the few is an oil painting of an old Negro man, "Uncle Israel," who was over a hundred years old when he died at Melrose. Another is of Choctaw Emma.

> another, similar. He ordered another painting, leaving it to me to select. I think I shall send him the magnolias I painted at Miss Cammie's [Henry, of Melrose]. It is a showy picture, and large enough for his office, for which he says he wants it. He is such a nice person that it is a pleasure to do anything for him.[9]

Carrie allowed two persons to purchase the majority of the paintings that she sold: Edith R. Stern of New Orleans and Lutcher Stark of Texas. Carrie painted a large number of iris for Stark when Virginia was invalided. Carrie explained: "I have to live."[10] She could not, though, crank out paintings commercially:

> Jo and Mr. Evans were all worked up over my painting LOTS of pictures. They think they will find a ready sale. There idea is fine—if it would work. But I cannot force that kind of thing—cannot just grind out pictures.[11]

Carrie's paintings were shown in a number of exhibitions.* In 1936 some of Carrie's work was shown at the Louisiana State Fair. In 1941 the Louisiana Art Commission, housed in the former state capitol, exhibited her work. She was invited to show her work at the Delgado Museum in New Orleans and at Louisiana State University. Her work was also shown in museums in Atlanta and Philadelphia. Enticing her to display her work at Centenary College, Director of Art Don Brown pleaded that Carrie would be in the company of Rembrandt, Whistler, and Audubon.[12] Such exhibitions seemed to have surprised Carrie. On July 22, 1958, she wrote:

> I always thought that some day I would sit down in the shades of Briarwood, and enjoy a nice quiet old age! Instead, I keep getting more and more involved. . . . They are having an exhibit of my work at the college at Natchitoches.[13]

*Dormon's work continues to be exhibited. On September 22, 1989, Longue Vue (House and Gardens, 7 Bamboo Road, New Orleans, Louisiana) hosted a reception to open a display entitled "Art in Flowers." Fifty-two watercolors and one oil owned by the estate of Mr. and Mrs. Edgar B. Stern were featured.

An exhibit at Northwestern State University in July 1958 featured Dormon's work. Among the thirty-one pieces were watercolors of various flowers, the pastels from the state planting projects, and the oil of Uncle Israel.[14]

In 1964 The Rachel McMasters Miller Hunt Botanical Library, Carnegie Institute of Technology, Pittsburgh, Pennsylvania, presented an "Exhibition of Contemporary Botanical Art and Illustration." George H. M. Lawrence, director, extended Carrie the invitation to exhibit; Carrie was the only woman in the group of 72 invited to this showing.[15]

Photography was another of Carrie's artistic endeavors. Carrie had amassed great numbers of photographs as she travelled about the state. She used many of her own photographs to illustrate the articles she wrote and the lectures she delivered. Most of Carrie's photographs, like her paintings, were of plants and trees. She photographed the state flower, magnolia grandiflora; piaroppus crassipos, water hyacinths; and golden rod and wild asters growing together.

In addition, other writers solicited her photographs for their use. William Lanier Hunt wrote:

> The immediate reason for this present letter is to say that in my book, I am anxious to have at least one photograph from the hands of each of the gardening authorities, botanists, and lovers of nature in general. I hope to get one from Dr. Hume, one from Dr. White, one from Harper who did the Bartram volume, one from Dr. Brown, and so on. I especially liked the photograph you published in *Home Gardening* some years ago of that swamp or marsh with Hymenocallises blooming in it—the great mass of them. Is the negative available so that I could have a print made?. . .
>
> Then, do you have other photographs of native material which you would be willing to sell me? I would want only the use of the negative for one print, so you would retain the negative in each case unless you happen to have some negatives you wish to sell.[16]

The British Iris Society asked to borrow Carrie's color slides of Louisiana Iris. Pictorial Publishing Company requested photographs to be used in a school encyclopedia.[17] Companies like Camera Clix of New York requested her photographs for their calendars and greeting cards. In sending Camera Clix samples of her photographic work, Carrie explained her approach: "The thing that make mine a little different is that I compose each one as carefully as if I were painting a landscape. It happens that I have painted landscapes for 30 years."[18] Yet Carrie did not always have total success. After several attempts to capture the pink color of the New Orleans iris, Carrie lamented: "For some strange reason, they always turn out lavendar. Makes me ?7'63#0!!"[19]

Carrie's artistic aim was always high. Insisting on honesty, she rarely used poses. Referring to an idyllic angling photograph, she boasted: "It was NOT posed! I had the good luck to stumble on it when I went over a bank to take [a picture of] the flowering hawthorne. Everyone who has seen it thinks it is *somep'n*."[20] She had a collection of Southern scenes, including photographs of cane fields, rice fields, and cotton fields. In describing one of her field pictures to a publishing company, she explained: "A cotton field (no manor house in *it—they don't plant cotton in front of the manor house* !!!)"[21]

Carrie was not a commerical artist. Her sketches, paintings, prints, and photographs served to advance her other interests and causes. Through her artistic endeavors, she had again accomplished her dream: "Before I lie down in peace to sleep, I should like to feel that I have had a part in saving some of the beauty with which God so kindly clothes this planet."[22]

Notes

1. Francois Mignon, "Plantation Memo," Alexandria *Daily Town Talk*, December 20, 1971.

2. Caroline Dormon, typed journal entry, January 14, 1938, Caroline Dormon Collection, Cammie G. Henry Research Center, Watson Memorial Library, Northwestern State University, Natchitoches, Louisiana, Folder 977.

3. Caroline Dormon, article dated January 23, 1935, Melrose Scrapbook.

4. Caroline Dormon, letter to Joe Evans, October 25, Folder 403.

5. Notes, Folder 222.

6. James R. Harlow, letter to Caroline Dormon, January 6, 1962, Folder 235.

7. Notes, Folder 71.

8. Caroline Dormon, typed journal entry, January 6, 1937, Folder 977.

9. *Ibid.*

10. Caroline Dormon, letter to Elizabeth Lawrence, March 11, 1959, Elizabeth Lawrence Collection, #25.

11. Caroline Dormon, typed journal entry, January 14, 1937, Folder 977.

12. Noted, Folder 207.

13. Caroline Dormon, letter, July 22, 1958, Folder 1131.

14. Notes, Folder 1089.

15. Notes, Folder 1258.

16. William Lanier Hunt, letter to Caroline Dormon, May 12, 1947, Folder 1243.

17. Notes, Folder 1119.

18. Caroline Dormon, letter to Camera Clix, April 4, 1946, Folder 1119.

19. Caroline Dormon, letter to Geddes, June 30, 1947, Folder 101.

20. Caroline Dormon, letter to Camera Clix, April 4, 1946, Folder 1119.

21. Caroline Dormon, letter, November 25, 1943, Folder 1119.

22. Caroline Dormon, typed journal entry, January 1, 1940, Folder 977.

BIRD CHATTING

As a child in Arcadia, Carrie had first learned about birds. "I can't remember when I began climbing trees to learn the mysterious variations in colors and patterns of birds' eggs, but I well remember inching out on a mossy limb of an old sweetgum to look into my first Blue-gray Gnatcatcher's nest. (My guardian angel had little time for loafing!)"[1]

Yet it was not until she and Virginia moved to Briarwood that Carrie was afforded the opportunity to closely study birds. Not only did the native plants attract birds, but Carrie also maintained feeding stations and bird baths. These amenities kept the birds in range so that Carrie could observe and paint them. "In a retaining wall below my window there are big flat rocks with numerous crevices. In these I stuff cornbread, and Wrens, Titmice and Nuthatches assume various attitudes while digging it out. With my sketchpad, I make pencil snapshots."[2] Some species were less accommodating. Dormon had more difficulty in pencil-snapping the Great Horned Owl and the Roadrunner. The owl required composite combinations, and the roadrunner refused to stand still.

Carrie made extensive notes of her observations. "White throats (sparrows) were late coming. I did not hear one till October 30, [1946]."[3] She watched large flocks of geese, seeking safe places to land for rest. She charted the supply of blackgum berries that fed robins and the "silent time" that preceded the song of the mockingbirds. Carrie sympathized with the birds as they moulted: "They must feel embarrassed at their dowdy appearance."[4] Her notes were detailed.

> May 11, 1937: Sparrow
> Under throat and breast oyster white, shading into grey-bluff at sides and under-tail-covert. Tail and wing feathers (long ones) soft brown. Entire color effect is soft and inconspicuous. Slender, long tail, conspicuously forked.[5]

Carrie listened as well as observed: "Heard a cardinal sing his full spring song today—not just once but over and over. Cannot remember such a thing occurring in November."[6] In a journal entry from January 3, 1937, Carrie recollected:

> While in the yard I heard the birds going to bed—a thing of which I never tire. They are never sweeter. From all over my woods come the ringing 'queets' of the white-throats—there must be hundreds of them. Right near by, in the laurel cherry, perhaps, I hear the goodnight whisper of Brown Thrasher. It is a ventriloquial sound and cannot be exactly placed. While I was closing the flower pit, Shelley (a mockingbird) came and sat right near me on the running rose (no cats were about). I began talking to him softly, and he drew nearer, puffed out his feathers, looked directly at me and turned his head from side to side. How he loves to be talked to! No other bird likes people quite so well.[7]

The following January Carrie wrote again of Shelley.

> When I chanced to look up, there sat my Shelley, not six feet over my head, singing away! But I'm sure no one ever heard such sotfly muted notes, yet so sweet and clear. I could not believe the song was coming from his throat until I watched it swell and tremble as he sang. When I talked softly to him, he turned his little head and looked down at me, then sang sweeter than ever. I know it was meant *just for me*.[8]

The camaraderie felt between Carrie and her birds grew. "A fine warbler has begun meeting me at the back door and eating from my hand."[9] Carrie allowed birds to fly in and out of her house. Wrens even built nests in her room. Carrie described other assistance she provided to the birds:

> Every year a saucy titmouse plucks hair from the hide-bottomed chair on the porch and gathers shreddy bark from the cedar posts. Today I was sitting very quietly on the log-seat between two of these posts, looking at a book, when a titmouse plumped down on the floor in front of me. He tilted his eye up at me and said, "Chi-cha-cha-cha,' in a most impudent manner. Then he flew

> from post to post, making a survey from every vantage point. Evidently my uncombed and fuzzy hair looked useful, for he planted himself firmly on my head, braced his feet, and began pulling it out by the beakful. 'Pop!' went the roots as they came out of their tiny sockets. I suppose I would be wearing a wig, but I just had to call Sister to come see (I wanted a witness to this performance), and the robber flew away. I wish I could see that nest.[10]

Carrie once defined excitement as watching wrens hatch in the bracket on the back porch. In fact, Carrie's notations were occasionally superseded by her unbridled joy at viewing her beloved.

> One day in spring I drove up in front of my house when a whole flock of Gold Finches flew up from the ground. I stopped my car and sat breathless. In a very few minutes they came back down and went on feeding on grass seeds. It looked as if someone had scattered bright-yellow flowers over the ground. Their color is purest aureolin, seldom as beautiful in paintings as it really is.[11]

Some of Carrie's observations, though, caused her alarm. She was distressed at declining numbers of birds, especially when the government appeared blameworthy. In 1935 she wrote Henry Wallace, United States secretary of agriculture.

> I was astonished to read that there was a possibility of Congress granting a thirty-day hunting season on ducks—after the repeated solemn warnings of the Biological Survey.
>
> This letter is from one who has spent her life in Louisiana, probably the greatest concentration ground of migratory waterfowl (particularly ducks and geese) in the world. And for many years I have watched, with a feeling of despair, the gradual decrease of these splendid creatures of the air . . . which were so plentiful in the early days of Louisiana that historians say the air would actually darken for hours by their flight. . . .

> I cannot believe that Congress will be influenced by the hollow noise so transparently coming from the makers of ammunition (and this is not intended for wit!) and allow an open season on waterfowl.
>
> I have no personal interest in this matter, except that I have always worked for the conservation of our splendid natural resources and I hate to see a things that is fine and beautiful vanish forever from the earth.[12]

Carrie questioned parents who provided their children with guns but did not teach them "what NOT to shoot." She was dismayed at the use of insecticides such as D. D. T., particularly since the argument for its use was that it was inexpensive. "Can anything be 'cheap' that wipes out our precious heritage of wildlife?"[13] Despite the birds' natural enemies like armadilloes, snakes, foxes, and cats,* Carrie believed "Homo sapiens is the greatest threat to our beloved birds."[14]

Weather was another enemy of the birds:

> Birdbaths frozen up solid this morning! The poor little birds are so pitiful, sliding around on the ice, so I took out a kettle of hot water to melt it. Few people realize that birds must have water as well as food.[15]

Birds and gardens were a natural combination in Carrie's mind, and one without the other was "unthinkable." Hearing a blue bird warble or red birds sing, Carrie believed, sent a gardener looking for a spade. Carrie compared the beauty of birds to the beauty of blossoms. "What flower can show the rare blue of the Indigo Bunting?"[16] Carrie labeled hummingbirds the "jewels" of gardens.[17]

Often Carrie spoke methaphorically of herself as bird. In a note to a friend she wrote: "Am puny—wings dragging."[18] Bird watching offered the cure. Invited to spend time with relatives, Carrie declined for "my birds

* Even the animals that were enemies of the birds often found friendship from Carrie. She maintained a cordial rapport with a speckled king snake which she named Hezikiah. A fox also frequented the grounds near Carrie's log home. "A beautiful fox visits us occasionally—licks up crumbs I put down for the birds. No doubt he licks up birds, too, and probably I should shoot him. But how can I extinguish that liquid flame."[19]

Courtesy Northwestern State University

A sketch by Caroline Dormon.

have come back, and how I enjoy them."[20] She prescribed bird watching to others: "Get somebody to make you a big bird feeder and hang it to a pecan limb or set a post and put it on that. You have no idea what a joy it can be."[21] And it was joy for Carrie. Upon discovering that a wren had not lost its mate, she posted a letter to share her delight: "The wren is NOT a widower! I watched and both went in the basket—the darlings."[22]

As in other areas of natural resources, Carrie gained professional respect. Clarence R. Stone, a 1936 visiting instructor at L. S. U., asked her to contribute to a series he had planned on Southern life. He wished her to write about the summer tanager.[23] In addition to specific requests such as this, Carrie contributed numerous articles to garden magazines and newspaper columns. Many of these articles, particularly those written for the *Shreveport Times*, formed a collection Carrie titled *Bird Talk* and published in 1969.

In *Bird Talk* Carrie prefaced: "There are just little chats, telling the things that I have learned by living intimately with birds throughout a long life."[24] Yet the book is both chatty and descriptive. For example, Carrie delineated differences among birds:

> The Yellow-throated Vireo is easily distinguished from the others [vireos] by the fact that the throat and breast are yellow. The back is olive, there are two white wing bars. . . . He is not often seen, for he is something of a treetop bird. His 'talk' is similar to that of the Red-eyed, but is lower in pitch and not incessant.[25]

Carrie described the eggs of the birds, for she interjected "One who has never peered into a bird's nest has missed the most delightful thrill of birding!"[26] She called the eggs of the Brown Thrasher "freckled" and the eggs of the Oriole marked with black "as if they were scrawled with pen and ink."[27] The eggs of the Wood Peewee, she characterized as "almost unbelievable."

> They are white, but the shell is so thin the color of the yolk shines through, giving them a pinkish glow. Then there is a wreath around the larger end in various shades of lavender and brown.[28]

Carrie provided interesting information about many of the species. She related name origins. "The Choctaw name for Mockingbird means 'bird of many tongues.' "[29] "The brilliant Baltimore Oriole gets his name from the family colors of Lord Baltimore, orange-yellow and black."[30] She offered a sandhill interpretation of the song of the Chuck-will-widow's: " 'chip-fell-out-o-the-white-oak,' accent on first and last words."[31] And she instructed:

> The person who named the Screech Owl should be sued for libel. The little fellow's cry bears no resemblance to a 'screech,' but is a soft, sad, quavering wail. An old myth that it is a sign of death causes superstitious folk to turn a shoe upside down or turn a sock! Many persons say it 'gives them the creeps,' but when one realizes it is a lovesong it is more acceptable.[32]

In describing the birds, Carrie frequently used human characteristics. She spoke of the Pine Warbler as "modest" but labeled the Redstart as vain: "There seems little doubt that exquisite Redstart is conscious of his beauty, for he is constantly lifting his wings and spreading his tail to display their bands of bright red."[33] She designated the Wren as "a model husband" but the Yellow-billed Cuckoo "a sloppy homemaker [whose] nest is merely a handfull of twigs thrown together, and one wonders why the eggs don't fall through."[34] Speaking of the charm of the Carolina Wren, Carrie referred to the bird as " 'she'—so dainty-looking, so full of delightful whimsies. Others must have felt this, for there is the old affectionate name 'Jenny Wren.' "[35] *Bird Talk*, like Carrie's other books, was warmly received.

Even in the last years of her life as her health and, consequently, her mobility were diminished, she found comfort in her bird friends. "Alas, my trampling days are over—a bad heart and a crippled hip—but my window by the fire looks out on a beautiful wild woodland where I can sit and watch birds."[36]

"GUESS WHO I AM?"*

I wear a cap,
And trees I tap,
But there's a meaning to every rap;
If 'twere not for me
You'd soon see
Worms a-crawling on every tree.

I'm big and loud,
I like a crow;
My coat is bright and gay.
To get a meal
I sometimes steal—
It's very wrong they say.

The darling of the woods am I,
Singing as the days go by;
With my speckled breast,
I'm easily guessed—
I'll wait right here till you try.

Just put me up a box or a gourd,
And I will surely pay my board.
As I go skimming all day long,
I'll give you a laugh instead of a song.

*Folder 767. Verses created by Caroline Dormon for school children. Answers: red-head, blue-jay, wood-thrush, martin.

Notes

1. Caroline Dormon, Bird Talk (Baton Rouge: Claitor's Publishing Division, 1969), p. 35.

2. Caroline Dormon, on display, Briarwood.

3. Caroline Dormon, handwritten notes divided by species, Caroline Dormon Collection, Cammie G. Henry Research Center, Watson Memorial Library, Northwestern State University, Natchitoches, Louiaiana, Folder 870.

4. Caroline Dormon, typed journal entry, August 15, 1937, Folder 977.

5. *Ibid.*

6. Caroline Dormon, handwritten journal entry, November 29, 1950, Folder 952.

7. Caroline Dormon, typed journal entry, January 3, 1937, Folder 977.

8. Caroline Dormon, typed journal entry, January 20, 1938, Folder 977.

9. Caroline Dormon, handwritten journal entry, February 2, 1965, Folder 952.

10. Caroline Dormon, typed journal entry, Saturday, May 1938, Folder 977.

11. Caroline Dormon, on display, Briarwood.

12. Caroline Dormon, letter to Henry Wallace, August 20, 1935, Folder 1152.

13. Caroline Dormon, on display, Briarwood.

14. Caroline Dormon, on display, Briarwood.

15. Caroline Dormon, letter to Francois Mignon, December 6, 1970, Melrose Collection, Folder 13.

16. Caroline Dormon, typed manuscript titled "A Garden Without Birds?" Folder 761.

17. Caroline Dormon, quoted in Natchitoches *Times*, February 2, 1967.

18. Caroline Dormon, letter to Sudie Lawton, on display at Briarwood.

19. Caroline Dormon, handwritten journal entry, January 20, 1954, Folder 952.

20. Caroline Dormon, letter, on display at Briarwood.

21. Caroline Dormon, letter, on display at Briarwood.

22. Caroline Dormon, letter to Sudie Lawton, December 1, 1961, on display at Briarwood.

23. Clarence R. Stone, letter to Caroline Dormon, July 7, 1936, Folder 964.

24. Caroline Dormon, *Bird Talk*, p. 2.

25. Caroline Dormon, *Bird Talk*, p. 34.

26. Caroline Dormon, *Bird Talk*, p. 36.

27. *Ibid.*

28. *Ibid.*

29. Caroline Dormon, *Bird Talk*, p. 85.

30. Caroline Dormon, *Bird Talk*, p. 40.

31. Caroline Dormon, *Bird Talk*, p. 55.

32. Caroline Dormon, *Bird Talk*, p. 58.

33. Caroline Dormon, *Bird Talk*, p. 55.

34. Caroline Dormon, *Bird Talk*, p. 71.

35. Caroline Dormon, *Bird Talk*, p. 60.

36. Caroline Dormon, handwritten journal entry, January 1, 1960, Folder 952.

"THE CHILDREN OF NATURE"

Carrie had learned about native Americans from her Papa who called the Indians "the children of nature." Papa had books and pamphlets which he shared with her. During the summer vacations spent at Briarwood, Carrie roamed the hills and woods and ponds just "like a little Indian."[1]

Carrie's interest in ethnology grew. She obtained additional materials from the Bureau of American Ethnology, Smithsonian Institution, and began corresponding with its director, John R. Swanton. At Carrie's invitation, Swanton visited Louisiana in order to study native American life. When he came in August of 1930, Carrie was recovering from an illness; Virginia chauffeured Swanton to surrounding areas, including the Dormons' hometown of Arcadia.[2] Carrie penned Swanton: "I am much better and will certainly be able to *talk*, if not able to go *Fording* about the country."[3]

Swanton and Dormon continued to correspond, sharing their findings and their questions and supporting each other's work. In 1932 Carrie urged Senator Edwin F. Broussard and the Senate Finance Committee not to interfere with the publication of the Bureau of Ethnology.

> . . . In a discussion some time ago, a southern senator (*not* from Louisiana, I am glad to say) referred to Bulletin 47, by Dr. John Swanton, as a 'useless paper.' Now the good senator was simply uninformed in this matter. I have read all of Dr. Swanton's bulletins, and they are both interesting and valuable. He has done more than any other one person to preserve the history of a lost people, our own Southern Indians.[4]

Carrie was not merely campaigning for a friend; she was campaigning for all who might learn from the Smithsonian publications about Southern Indians. Carrie knew there was a dearth of such material, for she had received inquiries from schools and organizations asking where such information could be found.

Carrie requested materials and maps that told of Southern Indian life, and she studied the language of Southern tribes, such as the Chitimacha. She especially studied a remnant of a tribe near the village of Charenton on

Bayou Teche. When she visited the Chitimacha tribe, the ancient chief told her he had known of her visit because the Yellow Bird sang "Good people coming."[5] She was intrigued by the three women of the tribe who made double-walled cane baskets, the making of which was a lost art. In "The Last of the Cane Basket Makers," an article which appeared in *Holland's* in October 1931, Carrie introduced these people and their art:

> . . . This part of Bayou Teche is still known as Indian Bend, and on these curving banks there live the few that are left of this ancient tribe. . . .
>
> From Indian hemp, a common weed, and the inside bark of mulberry, they wove a strong cloth. From these same materials they made ropes and packet carriers. But in the weaving of baskets, they displayed the greatest skill. Their basketry reached such a degree of development that it might well be classed among the higher arts. Most remarkable of all, they still retain this art. . . .
>
> The Chitimacha woman still goes to the bayou bank and cuts her green canes, strips them, and brings them home. This is hard work, but it is only the beginning. Seated on a bench, she holds a four-foot length of the reed in her bare hands and, with a quick twist of the wrists, splits it open. Now, ripe cane is very hard, but with the aid of her teeth, she divides it into smaller strips. When all are the right width, she takes a sharp knife and splits them the flat way, making them very thin. . .
>
> The Chitimacha specialty is the making of double-walled baskets, and in this their art has reached its peak development. With very fine splints, the maker begins at the bottom, inside, works up to the top; turns back down and weaves the outside, finishing at the bottom. With deft, quick motions, the left-over ends of splints are broken off, leaving a smooth finish. When completed, it is impossible to detect a beginning or an ending, so perfect is the workmanship. . . .
>
> The patterns are lovely, and there are dozens of them. Each has a name, and nothing better demonstrates the whimsical imagination of the Indian. Perhaps, in the long ago, each had its origin in some myth or legend. There is *napshkahkiti*, 'Turtle's

> Necklace'—and it does resemble a looped string of beads. Delightful, too, is Bear's Earrings. The reasons for the naming of Rabbit Teeth, Mouse Track, Blackbird Eyes, and Worm Track are a little more obvious. A large white circle with round dark center is Cow eyes. A beautiful winding pattern is *naxtua-ahki*, 'Alligator Entrails.'[6]

Carrie visited other tribes too. Virginia, Carrie, and a young nephew visited Eastern Cherokee in North Carolina. She found Eastern Cherokee in North Carolina who could not speak English. They were still making authentic paddle-stamped ware (the ware broke easily because, Carrie hypothesized, it was improperly fired).

Her primary interest, though, remained in more local Indian history and life, particularly the Caddo tribes of southwestern Arkansas, northwestern Louisiana, and northeastern Texas. She spent many years studying the ceramics of the Caddo tribes. She had viewed interesting pieces at aboriginal sites and in private collections. Carrie prepared an article "Caddo Pottery." *Art and Archaeology* published the article in its May-April 1934 issue. It was the first article to be published on the subject.[7] For the first volume of Hodges Gardens *Magazette*, Carrie wrote a more general article about the Caddo people, calling them "The First Families along El Camino Real."[8]

In 1932 she was invited to attend a conference on southern pre-history sponsored by the National Research Council. In issuing the invitation, Carl E. Guthe explained that the conference was an attempt to bring together people who were interested in the early history of Southern Indians and that her presence would "add to the meeting."[9] Guthe had heard of Carrie's work with pottery designs and was interested in her classifications.

At the meeting Carrie asked Guthe to forward her a sample constitution of ethnological organizations. Others in Louisiana had similar interests: Fred Kniffen, from L. S. U.; U. B. and Jo Evans; Edward Neild of Shreveport. Carrie and the others envisioned a state archaeological association,* an organization open to any with an interest in Southern ethnology; a central museum to house displays; a periodical to disseminate

* An association was formed, the Academy of Natural Sciences. In 1945 its name was changed to Shreveport Society for Nature Study. The members worked to have Poverty Point established as a state monument and park.

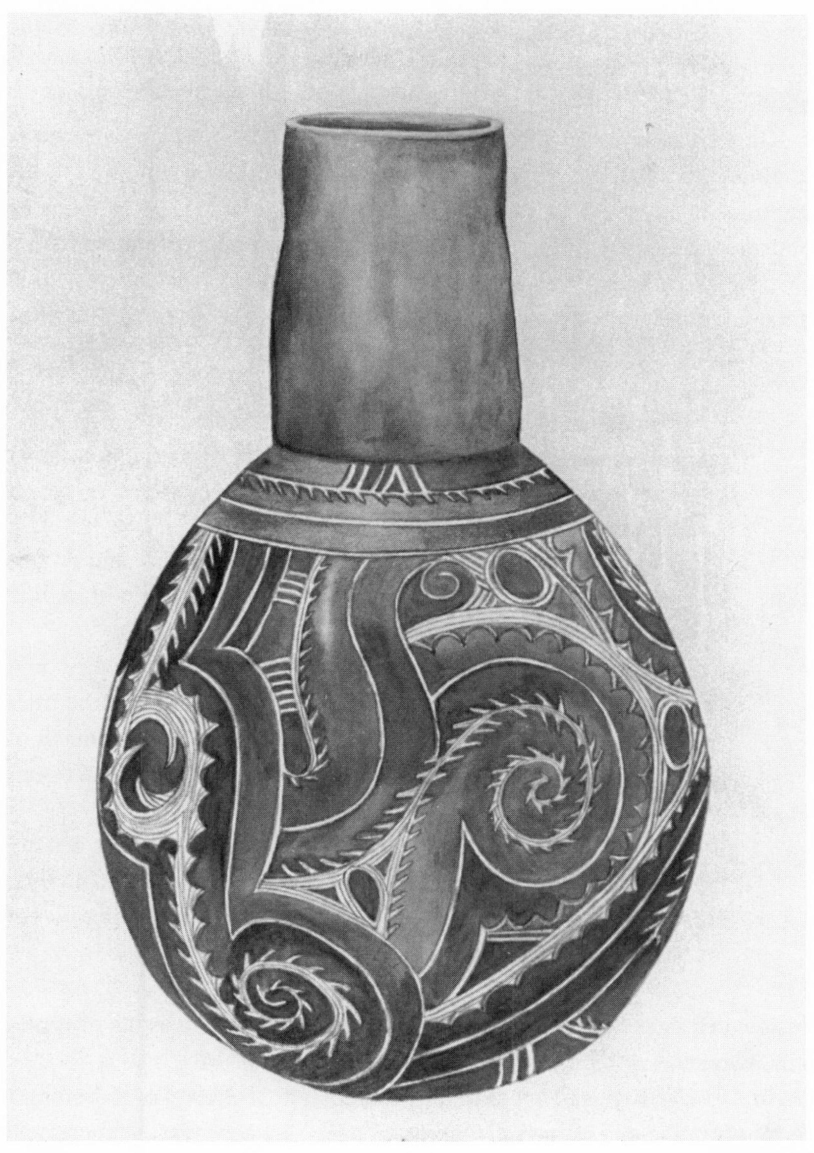

Courtesy Northwestern State University

Caroline Dormon's sketch of an Indian artifact.

information; and a systematic program to survey state mounds.[10] Carrie hoped that a state association could help educate the public to the importance of archaeology and, therefore, lessen the capricious digging of aboriginal sites.

Carrie championed other state-directed efforts. The Work Projects Administration had provided laborers for digs. In 1941, when most of the attention was turned to national defense, Carrie particularly became concerned about the sites. Not only were WPA laborers removed from mound explorations, but also Carrie feared that army maneuvers would damage the mounds themselves. Carrie wrote General C. B. Hodges, president of L. S. U. to enlist his help:

> The pottery, etc., left by the Natchez, Caddo, and a prehistoric people presently identified by the so-called 'Marksville culture,' seem to indicate that the cradle of primitive culture in North America was right here in this state.
>
> The work on this pre-history has just been begun, and no one knows when one particular mound will give us an important link in the chain. . . .
>
> There is certainly no doubting Louisiana's loyalty and patriotism, and it is enough to have millions of young pine trees destroyed—that is unavoidable. But the generals in command of the two armies in the state at this time, can command that our Indian mounds and other remains be left intact. . . .
>
> Knowing your connection with the army, I thought a letter from you to generals Kreuger and Lear would be effective, especially as you are president of the institution carrying on the investigation of these archaeological subjects.[11]

President Hodges forwarded a copy of Carrie's letter as well as his own plea to the two generals.

In 1954 Carrie was appointed to the Historical Sites Commission of the North Louisiana Historical Association.[12] This commission sponsored commemoration of important sites such as marking the grave of Dr. John Sibley at Natchitoches. In 1954 Dr. G. W. McGinty, president of the NLHA, invited Carrie to make a presentation at the society's meeting.[13]

During the late fifties and the early sixties, Carrie became increasingly more concerned about indiscriminate excavations. In August of 1961, an article in the *Shreveport Times* reported excavation in a burial ground in the Tunica Reservation. Carrie was outraged. In a letter to the Department of Geology and Anthropology at L. S. U., she reprimanded, she instructed, and she implored.

> . . . This is *not* archaeology, but desecration of a cemetery belonging to living people.
>
> What a howl would be raised if archaeologists were to start digging in Bonaventure Cemetery (Savannah), or at the St. Louis Cathedral in New Orleans! Both of these contain graves as old as the one under discussion.
>
> 'Probably dating back to the time when the Conquistadores roamed the Gulf Coast. . . .' What nonsense! The last appearance of the Spanish explorers was about 1540—when the pitiful remnants of De Soto's army drifted down the Mississippi. (This romantic touch may have been added by the reporter.). . .
>
> Last, if this digging is on the Tunica Reservation, as stated, it is federal property, and disturbing a burial ground is a federal offense.[14]

Carrie, unflagging and unselfish in such efforts, subordinated her own archaeological work to assist others in their archaeological searches. In 1933 she first helped F. M. Setzler, assistant curator of Archeology, Smithsonian Institution, and then similarly assisted James A. Ford. Both men were particularly interested in the Hopewell-like culture of Louisiana and the Marksville area. Carrie shared notes and showed them various sites.[15]

In February 1937, a Yale linguist Mary Haas Swadesh, stayed three days at Briarwood to learn what Carrie knew about the language of Southern Indians. Carrie noted the visit in her journal:

> . . . Mrs. Swadesh is making a highly specialized study of Southern Indian languages. She is good—can even pronounce those outrageous Chitimacha words, filled with consonant

> sounds—some of which our alphabet is quite inadequate to express. She and I had a grand time discussing Southern Indians.[16]

Carrie was deluged with requests from enthusiasts and educators. Essae M. Culver, first Louisiana state librarian, inquired about the word for *love* in the Natchitoches Indian dialect. Carrie replied:

> Sad to relate, Natchitoches is one of the lost languages. The last Natchitoches Indian died years ago, and no one had recorded a vocabulary. We know that the Natchitoches was a Caddoan tribe, and that is all.
>
> The same is true of Ouachita. I have read several stories of the meaning of *Ouachita—such* as 'singing waters,' etc., but it is all bosh. Dr. Swanton has searched many old records and has tried to work it out linguistically, but to no avail. . . .
>
> When the correct interpretation is not known, it is unfortunate that people concoct one of their own! And even when the meaning *is* known, a lot of foolish stories are published. For example, I have read a pretty legend about the name of Pascagoula River, and that the name means 'The Singing River.'. . . Pascagoula is a Choctaw word meaning "The Bread People.' But Moran Tudury, in his present story in the Country Gentleman—' 'The Singing River'—just accepted this interpretation. . . . His story makes pleasant reading, but it could have been equally so, and stuck to facts. In Louisiana, the *truth* is more fascinating than *any* fiction!
>
> Am sorry there is nothing to be done about this word.[17]

Carrie's interest in Indians went beyond the historical. She possessed a profound concern for their welfare, a welfare she felt had been jeopardized by systematic cheating and robbing. She had read the histories and contemporary analyses. She was active in Indian-rights movements, rallying support for justice and chastising those who oppressed the cause. She had approbation for John Collier, commissioner of Indian Affairs, and his policies to give back the Indian grazing lands and to allow the Indian degrees of self-government. Carrie feared that a movement led by senators from Oklahoma and South Dakota was merely a "sneak attack" aimed at taking land from the Indians and giving it to cattlefarmers.[18] She characterized their senate report as "the most dastardly attack on Indians that has been known since pioneer days—days when there was at least the excuse of actual conflict."[19] Carrie asked Senator John Overton to interpose:

> While our great President and the Congress are burdened with the awful responsibility of winning this war [1945], an attempt is being made to sabotage the wonderful work of our present Bureau of Indian Affairs. In order to slip these measures through without attracting the attention of those who want to protect the Indian, a number of separate bills have been prepared, making it much more difficult to catch them. The most significant fact in the whole affair is that these bills—and the Senate report which preceded them—are all the work of three or four senators from those western states which have systematically robbed the Indians for more than a hundred years. It would seem that the movement is fostered by Senator Burton Wheeler. . . .
>
> If those of us who stand for decency and fair play do not watch diligently, these measures will pass, and the Indian will be tossed to the wolves once more. I know we can count on your support in this affair.[20]

Carrie included in her letter to Overton a statement of the case, citing government reports and authorities on Indians.

She wrote newspapers, admonishing editors for anti-Indian reportage. She chastised editors for inflamatory headlines such as "Indian Uprising Feared." As advisory chair of Indian welfare for the Louisiana Federation of Women's Clubs, Carrie worked to advance the rights of Indians by distributing information to local chapters.[21] She also worked with the Daughters of the American Revolution on Indian concerns, making talks to various clubs to enlarge support.[22] She saw results: "Louisiana is reaping some benefit from the general move to help the Indian. We now have four Indian schools in Louisiana—Chitimacha, Houma, Choctaw, and Koasati. We need one more, Tunica, near Marksville."[23]

Her efforts were not merely exerted for a people, but also for persons. She wrote governmental agencies on behalf of individuals like Della Bel

Krausem, who was being sued by the government over title to lands. She took particular interest in the physical health of these "children of nature." In a letter to her friend A. R. Johnson, Carrie described a visit to a sick Indian child:

> At first she just looked at me with those suffering dark eyes—there was no response whatever. But I had brought her one of those color books—big outlines of birds, animals, and children—and a box of crayolas. Quietly I turned the pages and began talking about the animals and birds. Then I colored a blue bird, holding it so that she could watch me. When I looked back at her, her face was slight with interest. I left her happily coloring a little chicken.[24]

Carrie wished to share her knowledge of the Indians in order to increase public awareness of their plight and public support for improvement of their condition. Not only had Carrie taken voluminous archaeological notes, but she had also recorded Indian narratives. Describing her material, she explained:

> . . . I am not telling the fanciful stories one often hears of Indian maidens leaping off bluffs for unrequited love. Those are NOT Indian legends, but tales fabricated by the white man and hung onto the Indian. These that I tell are the real myths and legends handed down by word of mouth for generations.[25]

In addition to having taken notes before the "old ones passed on," Carrie believed she had the voice for the stories: "I speak the language of the wild things—which is necessary when writing of aboriginal Americans."[26] Carrie submitted to various publishing houses several stories, including "Katcilutci, A Creek Indian Boy," "Hi-Chach, A Caddo Boy," "Tooski, A Tunica Boy," "Red Boots and Deer Runner," "Sequoia, A Cherokee Boy," Dr. John A. Swanton previewed the stories and provided the following statement for Carrie to send to publishers:

> I have read your collection of stories with a great deal of pleasure. The selection is admirable—the best for popular usage for the region covered with which I am acquainted—and they give a very true idea of the myths and tales current among the Indians of the Gulf area in aboriginal times and during the subsequent four centuries of white contact. Their authentic character and delightful manner in which they are told should insure them a large audience.[27]

Despite this praise and the stories themselves, several publishers complained that the market was overcrowded with Indian stories; Carrie countered that the market included no stories about Southern Indians. She did not relent, saying: "I can't bear it if I don't get to place all this interesting material I have gathered in the hands of children."[28]

After a number of rejections from publishers, Carrie reached an agreement with Claitor's Book Store of Baton Rouge. In 1967 two of the Indian stories, "Red Boots and Deer Runner" and "Hi-Chach," and a brief history of the Chitimacha and the Caddo were bound in a small volume titled *Southern Indian Boy* wherein pleasure and knowledge are commingled. William Lanier Hunt reviewed the book in his column "Southern Gardens."

> Few of us who read and enjoy Caroline Dormon's books about plants realize that she is one of the South's few experts on the Indians, too. On my last visit to Caroline, she showed me some of her Indian baskets and explained their designs to me.
>
> A lifetime of study and visits with her Indian friends make Caroline Dormon the Southerner who knows most about our Southern Indians. Her book, recently published, about two Louisiana Indian boys is one of the most delightful books ever published on the subject.[29]

Notes

1. Caroline Dormon, letter to Mr. Leslie, November 11, 1955, Caroline Dormon Collection, Cammie G. Henry Research Center, Watson Memorial Library, Northwestern State University, Natchitoches, Louiaiana, Folder 1128.

2. Notes, Folders 1359 and 1360.

3. Caroline Dormon, letter to Dr. John R. Swanton, August 5, 1930, Folder 1360.

4. Caroline Dormon, letter to Senator Edwin F. Broussard, March 6, 1932, Folder 1147.

5. Unnamed Indian Chief, quoted by Caroline Dormon, letter to The David McKay Company, June 23, 1943, Folder 978.

6. Caroline Dormon, "The Last of the Cane Basket Markers," Holland's, October 1931, Folder 792.

7. Caroline dormon, "Caddo Pottery," Art and Archaeology, May-April 1934, Folder 733.

8. Caroline Dormon, "The First Families along El Camino Real," Hodges Gardens Magazet, Folder 733.

9. Carl E. Guthe, letter to Caroline Dormon, November 15, 1932, Folder 1447.

10. Notes, Folder 1393.

11. Caroline Dormon, letter to General C. B. Hodges, President L. S. U., August 31, 1941, Folder 1474.

12. D. H. Perkins, letter to Caroline Dormon, April 13, 1954, Folder 225.

13. G. W. McGinty, letter to Caroline Dormon, January 11, 1956, Folder 225.

14. Caroline Dormon, letter to Department of Geology and Anthropology at L. S. U., August 7, 1961, Folder.

15. Notes, Folders 1447 and 1449.

16. Caroline Dormon, typed journal entry, February 21, 1937, Folder 977.

17. Caroline Dormon, letter to Essae M. Culver, March 26, 1945, Folder 550.

18. Notes, Folder 1147.

19. Caroline Dormon, letter on display at Briarwood.

20. Caroline Dormon, letter to Senator John Overton, February 3, 1945, Folder 1148.

21. Notes, Folder 653.

22. Notes, Folder 641.

23. Caroline Dormon, letter to Senator Allen J. Ellender, August 5, 1937, Folder 1436.

24. Caroline Dormon, letter to A. R. Johnson, State Hospital Director, October 25, 1939, Folder 635.

25. Caroline Dormon, letter to Betsy, Friday, Folder 1482.

26. Caroline Dormon, letter to The David McKay Company, June 23, 1943, Folder 978.

27. Dr. John R. Swanton, letter to Caroline Dormon, Folder 357.

28. Caroline Dormon, typed journal entry, February 28, 1937, Folder 977.

29. William Lanier Hunt, "Southern Gardens," Folder 951.

DOCTOR DORMON

Caroline Dormon had never sought recognition, but her contributions did not go unrecognized. Recognition came from many areas. Carrie received medals in 1953, 1954, 1955, and 1958, from the American Iris Society and won the Mary Swords Deballion Award five times for introducing Louisiana native irises. She was elected to life membership in the John James Audubon Foundation and the Louisiana Society for Horticultural Research.

The Judson, Carrie's alma mater, selected Carrie for its Alumnae Award in 1959. The college presented Carrie with a silver bowl, a replica of a silver punchbowl on which all the names of recipients are engraved. Conwell A. Anderson, president of Judson, wrote Carrie that the college did not have a policy of awarding honorary doctorates but that the college was, nonetheless, proud of her. Information about Carrie's achievements was printed in the college newspaper, *Triangle*.[1]

In 1960 the Garden Club of American awarded her the Eloise Payne Luquer Medal for special achievement in the field of botany. Although Carrie did not attend the presentation held at Palm Beach, Florida, on April 7, she forwarded an acceptance note, a note which not only expressed her appreciation, but also which challenged others to the cause of conservation:

> It is with deepest regret that I cannot be with you today to accept the medal which you have so surprisingly awarded to me. All of my adult life I have gone quietly about the work that I love, with no expectation of awards or rewards, so when you gave this honor to me, it was a happy experience which gave a lift to my spirit. . . .
>
> Your club stands for accomplishment; therefore, I hope it is not inopportune for me to mention my life-long dream—to see many wild flower preserves [established] to save our fast-vanishing native flora. In his book *Magnolias of the World*, Millais (an Englishman!) gives more space to our own Magnolia macrophylla than to any other species. There are still a few groves of this

> spectacular flowering tree, but if one has been secured and set aside for preservation, I do not know of it.[2]

The American Horticultural Society honored Carrie with its 1961 citation for outstanding accomplishment in the field of amateur gardening. Carrie was not present for the presentation in Northampton, Massachusetts, but the citation read:

> To Caroline Dormon of Saline, Louisiana, for outstanding contribution to horticulture through her valuable information on flowering plants native to the Deep South, for her writings and extremely accurate drawings of the plants, and for her own garden, which is actually a sanctuary for the flora of the South.[3]

In 1962 Northwestern State College Alumni Association presented Carrie with honorary life membership. The Natchitoches Parish Library installed a fountain designed by Rivers Murphy, NSU. The abstract modular design suggests a floral arrangment.[4]

The Pelican Council of Girl Scouts asked Caroline to help establish a nature trail at Camp Wawbansee near Arcadia. During 1963 and 1964 Carrie and her friend Inez Conger planned the nature path. Not only did Carrie identify the plants and trees that should be included, she also donated and planted many of the species, including silverbell, wild hydrangea, cyrilla, and fringe tree. Informing Carrie of the council's decision to name the trail in her honor, Mrs. Ben Sur wrote: "Our highest hope is that as girls and leaders through the years walk this trail in search of peace and beauty, they also may be reminded to search for the high ideals you exemplify."[5]

In July 1964 an ad hoc committee was appointed to conside the nomination of Caroline Dormon for an honorary doctorate from Louisiana State University. That committee listed the following as the bases for her nomination:

1. Her publications as a botanist and botanical illustrator
2. Her services to forest conservation, in particular her promotion of Kisatchie National Forest

3. Her contributions to horticulture through publications, lectures, and successful experiments in hybridizing Louisiana irises.
4. Her services to archaeological and ethnological studies of the American Indians, especially as a member of the DeSoto Expedition Commission.[6]

By December 1964 L. S. U. had received numerous letters of support, including letters from Edgar Anderson, Missouri Botanical Gardens; Elizabeth Lawrence, author; George Lawrence, director of Botanical Library; Carnegie Institution; Frank Gladney, president of John James Audubon Foundation; Joel L. Fletcher, president of the University of Southwestern Louisiana.[7] The faculty of the School of Forestry and Wildlife Management unanimously voted its support, the faculty of the College of Arts and Sciences recommended that the Honorary Degree of Doctor of Science be conferred upon Dormon, and President John A. Hunter concurred. A citation was then proposed:

> Caroline Coroneos Dormon:
> For your valuable contributions to knowledge in the fields of botany, horticulture, and forestry;
> For your work as an educator who has kindled the interest and imagination of young and old throughout Louisiana and beyond;
> For your ability to combine beauty of expression through the media in painting and drawing with distinguished scientific achievement of the best Audubon tradition;
> For your furtherance of the cause of conservation in Louisiana through your influence on legislation and administration:
> Louisiana State University is proud to confer upon you the well-deserved degree of DOCTOR OF SCIENCE.[8]

On January 26, 1965, Carrie was awarded the honorary degree. She wrote a friend about the occasion: "I'm in a nervous jitter getting ready to go down for my 'coronation.' "[9]

Carrie received other recognition from her state. In 1966 Legislative Act 115 (H855 Corveil and Tarver) authorized the director of Parks and

Courtesy Northwestern State University

Doctor Dormon

Courtesy Northwestern State University

The Caroline Dormon Lodge.

LIVING MEMORIALS*

When I am dead,
Will someone plant a tree there where I lie?
Then dust shall stir to life again,
Become a party of beauty rich and infinite.
What rare fulfillment to become a tree!
To feel new snow upon my face
And wrestle strongly with outrageous winds;
To hold the sun against my cheek,
And live anew in birth of flowers each spring;
To gather to my breast the birds
That speak for me through lovely throats;
To reach above man's little frets and cares.
Then I shall touch God—
And yet keep hold on warm sweet earth I love.

* Poem written by Caroline Dormon for *Home Gardening for the South,* October 1945.

Recreation to name the lodge at Chicot State Park "The Caroline Dormon Lodge."[10]

In 1968 T. N. McMullan, director of Library, Louisiana State University, offered to name a collection in honor of Carrie: "I hope that you have made your will to include your collection so that we may have a Caroline Dormon Room. We will add to this room books on wild flowers and those that are native to the state."[11] Although Northwestern State University purchased many of the Dormon papers, some paintings and documents were given to the Louisiana State University library.

In addition to national and state recognition, Carrie also earned the appreciation of her own sand-hill neighbors. Nora, a black woman who worked for Carrie, once remarked: "You know Miss Carrie people does say you is peculiar."[12] Carrie won them over.

> Their attitude is delightful—I mean the neighbors—now. At first they strained their minds trying to understand what it was all about—a woman that spends all her time foolin' with bushes and weeds. At last they have just given me up as hopeless. They *know* I am crazy, but harmless so anything I do is all right. A really happy state of affairs.[13]

This happy state of affairs, though, was dimmed; for the last years of Carrie's life were punctuated with increasing health problems, especially a weak heart. Carrie, however, continued her campaigns. In 1966 in a letter to Lady Bird Johnson, Carrie explained: "My traveling days are over, so I am trying to accomplish what I can with my pen."[14] Carrie praised Mrs. Johnson for her national beautification and preservation programs. Carrie also expressed an anxiety:

> May I presume to suggest a word of warning? Nurserymen are picking up your idea, but they are urging the planting of dayliles, roses, etc. (Native roses are fine, but native species only.) In past years my own state suffered from this trouble. Nurserymen with a 'pull' got contracts to plant certain stretches of road—and simply dumped off their surplus stock. I know you can scarcely believe it, but they even planted arbor vitaes, of all things![15]

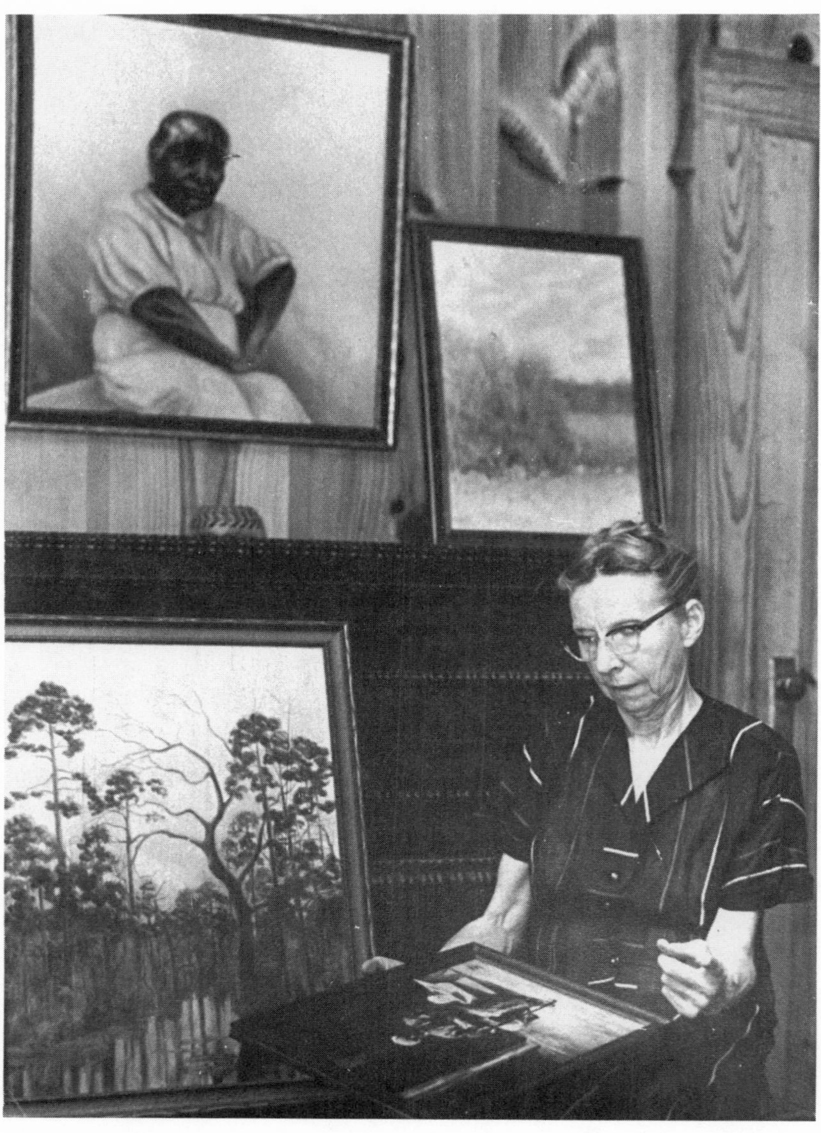

Courtesy of
John C. Guillet

Caroline Dormon with her paintings.

Courtesy of
John C. Guillet

Caroline Dormon at Briarwood.

Natural highway beautification was just one of many crusades of the final years. She wrote hundreds of letters championing such natural causes as predator control and reservoir projects. She wrote Senator Ernest Gruening of Alaska to ask him to intervene in a United States Corp of Engineers' proposal to flood a vast area of northern Alaska, a proposal which would have reduced the grazing lands of caribou, moose, bears, and dall sheep.[16] She protested the drainage of the Florida everglades, and she was at the forefront of a campgian against DDT.

> D. D. T. must go! No longer is it merely a matter of saving our songbirds. The reckless use of deadly pesticides is threatening our very lives . . . Scientists have even found D. D. T. in penguins in Antartica! It causes birds to lay infertile eggs, and this is one cause of the destruction of our eagles.[17]

Carrie's concerns were not limited to nature. She fought for issues involving foreign trade, domestic spending, war and peace. Writing the editor of the *Shreveport Times*, she characterized the presidency of Truman:

> . . . I am disappointed that you have not made a greater effort to deflate that unblieveable windbag Harry Truman.
>
> . . . He [Truman] states that he does not regret any decision he ever made! This is the index to his mentality and his moral fiber.
>
> Truman, by whose command Eisenhower and Patton held back our victorious armies and let our *dear allies*, the Russians, march into Germany ahead of us—thus giving us a divided Berlin and Germany today.
>
> Truman, who refused to *permit* us to win the war in Korea.
>
> Truman, who recalled the greatest general American has produced.
>
> Truman, who dropped the atom bombs on Japan, without giving her the chance to surrender; who did not even consult with MacArthur, though he was in charge of the Pacific area.
>
> These are just a few of the decisions he does NOT regret. . . .
>
> His bombastic boasting (and actual misstatement of facts) makes me blush to think that I once voted for him![18]

In 1970 Carrie wrote the editor of *The Christian Herald* to plea for religious tolerance and understanding:

> It shocks and grieves me that so many Christian people should still hold to the belief that evolution contradicts the Bible. This is stubborn and childish and causes Christianity to be ridiculed.
>
> The very idea of thinking that God's day is our puny man made day of twenty-four hours. Such conceit. . . .
>
> I live alone in my beautiful forest and feel very close to God in nature.[19]

Carrie enclosed an article "Darwin Was Not an Atheist" with her letter. In the article she wrote: "It seems infantile to dispute evolution, when the wonderful story is written in the primeval rocks for all to read. It should increase our reverence for ONE who could work out a plan so vast, so intricate, and so beautiful."[20]

These letters from 1970 are among the final pieces of correspondence from Carrie, for during the latter part of the year she suffered an attack of angina. During the very last months of her life, her heart was so weak that she was unable to remain at her beloved Briarwood in spite of the magnanimity of kind neighbors like Mae Nichols. Carrie had been born at Briarwood, and there she wished to die. She wrote: "I'd rather be dead than in one of the old folks' home! All those gabby old women!"[21] But her health was so precarious that her very last days were spent at Nursecare Nursing Home in Shreveport. She died there at 5:30 a. m. on November 23, 1971. Her body was interred at Briarwood Baptist Cemetery. A native dogwood guards her grave.

Notwithstanding the various awards, plaques, citations, and medals, Caroline Dormon received during her life, she was able to extend her contributions beyond her own life span. Near the end of her life, Carrie relinguished her beloved Briarwood.

Virtually on her death bed, Carrie summoned Richard Johnson to entrust him with the careship of Briarwood. Carrie had molded Richard for this careship. Seldom allowing anyone other than herself to dig among her flowers, she permitted Richard to dig, reminding him that digging could not be done with a straight back and admonishing him to get on "his prayer bones." Richard describes himself as "a squirrel Miss Carrie couldn't run off."[22]

Sudie Lawton and Arthur Watson of Natchitoches worked tirelessly with the legal transition of Briarwood. Within months after Carrie's death, Richard Johnson, his wife, Jessie, Lawton, and Watson had set in motion the restoration of Briarwood as well. Today Briarwood continues as a living monument to Doctor Dormon.

In a letter to Cammie Henry, Carrie wrote: "Well, at least I've had a full life, even if it did look very quiet and uneventful to others."[23]

"Quite and uneventful"—Caroline Coroneos Dormon almost singularly promoted the establishment of Kisatchie National Forest; she was the first female to be employed by the United States Forestry Department; she authored five books and innumerable articles; she was appointed by President Franklin Roosevelt as one of the five representatives to the De Soto Commission; she exhibited in water color and oil; she corresponded with national and international horticulturalists and botanists; she was honored by flower and botanical societies; she collected, grew, and hybridized native flora, including Louisiana iris; she was a teacher, an ethnologist, an archaeologist, a naturalist, and a generous preserver of native life who willed her lifelong home and land for future generations to enjoy.

Perhaps Carrie best describes her life in an application for a grant when she is asked to list her "Attainments" and "Plans for work": "It is difficult to know where my 'attainments' leave off, and my 'plans for work' begin. There is no beginning and no ending. It is my life."[24]

Notes

1. Notes, Caroline Dormon Collection, Cammie G. Henry Research Center, Watson Memorial Library, Northwestern State University, Natchitoches, Louiaiana, Folder 1092.

2. Caroline Dormon, typed note to be read at national meeting of The Garden Club of America, Palm Beach, Florida, April 7, 1960, Folder 1098.

3. Citation from The American Horticultural Society, 1961, Folder 1099.

4. Letters and Photographs on display at Briarwood.

5. Mrs. Ben Sur, letter to Caroline Dormon, Folder 457.

6. S. J. P. Chilton, W. G. Haag, W. J. Jokinen, R. deV. Williamson, and O. B. Wheeler, Faculty and Studies Committee, Minutes, December 5, 1964, Folder 1134.

7. Edgar Anderson, Elizabeth Lawrence, George Lawrence, Frank Gladney, and Joel L. Fletcher, letters of recommendation, Folder 1134.

8. Copy of inscription on citation for Dormon's honorary doctorate from L. S. U., Folder 1134.

9. Caroline Dormon, letter on display at Briarwood.

10. Notes, Folder 899.

11. T. N. McMullan, letter to Caroline Dormon, December 5, 1968, Folder 1087.

12. Nora Patterson, quoted by Caroline Dormon, letter to Elizabeth Lawrence, November 7, 1962, Elizabeth Lawrence Collection #29.

13. *Ibid.*

14. Caroline Dormon, letter to Lady Bird Johnson, October 7, 1966, Folder 1131.

15. *Ibid.*

16. Caroline Dormon, letter to Senator Ernest Gruening of Alaska, July 28, 1965, Folder 1151.

17. Caroline Dormon, Letter to Senator A. Ribicoff, January 22, 1969, Folder 1146.

18. Caroline Dormon, letter to Editor of Shreveport *Times*, July 5, 1960, Folder 1138.

19. Caroline Dormon, letter to Kenneth L. Wilson, Editor of *The Christian Herald*, June 2, 1970, Folder 746.

20. Caroline Dormon, typed "Darwin Was Not an Atheist," Folder 746.

21. Caroline Dormon, letter to Elizabeth Lawrence, December 6, 1967, Elizabeth Lawrence Collection #33.

22. Richard Johnson, Curator of Briarwood, Interview November 3, 1988.

23. Caroline Dormon, letter to Cammie Henry, December 2, 1970, on display at Briarwood.

24. Caroline Dormon, application for a Guggenheim Fellowship, 1942, Folder 1095.

Courtesy of
John C. Guillet

"Bring me what you will, but leave me my wide-open view of the sky, the wind on my face, sweet clean earth to dig in, the whir of wings . . . and all my 'gift of the wild things.'"*

*Caroline Dormon, typed journal entry, January 1, 1938, folder 977.

SELECTED BIBLIOGRAPHY OF ARTICLES BY CAROLINE DORMON

"Adventures in Louisiana Irises," *Bulletin of the Iris Society*, London, 1948.

"Adventures in Wild Flowers," *Garden*, Vol. 1, no. 1, March 1935, pp. 4-6.

"Arbor Day Program for Louisiana," Baton Rouge: Department of Conservation, Division of Forestry and United States Forest Service, 1928.

"Around the Calendar with Native Shrubs," *Holland's*, Vol. 53, no. 11, November 1934, pp. 26, 49.

"Autumn Color in the Landscape," *Holland's*, Vol. 56, no. 11, November 1937, pp. 26, 30.

"Birds: A Morning at the Feeding Tray," *Will H. Dilo League Monthly*, July 1928, p. 5.

"Blueprinting Wild Flowers," *Holland's*, June 1925.

"Bog Plants," *Home Gardening for the South*, vol. 2, no. 1, October 1941, pp. 4-5, 19.

"Botanical Ramblings," *Louisiana Society for Horticultural Research*, 1976.

"By Their Fruits," *American Iris Society Bulletin*, No. 108, January 1948, pp. 45-48.

"Caddo Pottery," *Art and Archaeology*, Vol. 35, no. 2, March-April 1934, pp. 59-68.

"Camping in the Kisatchie Wold," *Natchitoches Times*, July 26, 1929, p. 4.

"Carefree Camellias," *Home Gardening for the South*, vol. 7, no. 1, January 1947, pp. 18-19.

"Cities of Refuge," *Holland's*, December 1930.

"Consider the Virginicas," *American Iris Society Bulletin*, No. 118, July 1950, pp. 32-33.

"Crape-Myrtle Takes to the North," *American Home*, vol. 53, no. 6, May 1955, pp. 126-127.

"Distinctive Gardens," *Holland's*, vol. 55, no. 5, May 1936, p. 26.

"Evergreens," *Holland's*, December 1931.

Flowers Native to the Deep South. Baton Rouge: Claitor's Book Store, 1958.

Forest Trees of Louisiana. Baton Rouge: Louisiana Department of Conservation, Division of Forestry, 1941.

Forest Trees of Louisiana. Baton Rouge: Louisiana Department of Conservation, Division of Forestry, 1943.

Forest Trees of Louisiana. Baton Rouge: Louisiana Department of Conservation, Division of Forestry, no date, (Cover is colored illustration).

"Fragrant Gardens," *Holland's*, November 1931.

"Highway Beauty—Now," *Holland's*, vol. 52, no. 8, August 1933, p. 18.

"Highway Heritage," *Holland's*, January 1927.

"Highways Plus Trees," *Holland's*, April 1923.

"In Spring, Louisiana Beckons," *Louisiana Tourist Bulletin*, Vol. 4, no. 6, May 1941, pp. 12-13.

"Iris," *Holland's*, March 1931, pp. 31, 61, 63.

"Iris Journal 1948," *Home Gardening for the South*, Vol. 8, no. 8, September 1948, pp. 196-197, 211.

"Irises for the Rock Garden," *Home Gardening for the South*, Vol. 7, April 1947, pp. 100-101.

"It's Time You Tried the Louisiana Iris," *Flower Grower*, Vol. 36, August 1949, pp. 668-669.

"Just Evergreens," *Holland's*, February 1931.

"The Last of the Cane Basket Makers," *Holland's*, October 1931.

"Let's Plant Natives," *Louisiana Society for Horticultural Research*, 1965.

"Louisiana," in Kathryn S. Taylor's *A Traveler's Guide to Roadside Wild Flowers, Shrubs, and Trees, of the United States*, New York: Farrar, Strauss, and Company, 1949, pp. 105-106.

"Louisiana Iris," *The Garden Journal of the New York Botanical Garden*, Vol. 3, no. 2, March-April 1953, pp. 52-53.

"Louisiana Iris Journal, 1949," *Home Gardening for the South*, vol. 9, no. 9, October 1949, pp. 202-203, 216.

"Louisiana Iris Reaches Stardom," *Home Gardening for the South*, vol. 10, October 1950, pp. 224-225.

"Louisiana Iris Round-up," *Home Gardening for the South*, vol. 11, no. 7, July-August 1951, pp. 157, 180.

Louisiana Landscape. State Parks for Louisiana, published by Louisiana State Parks Association, no date.

"Louisiana, Our Garden," *Home Gardening for the South*, vol. 1, no. 6, March 1941, pp. 4, 15.

"The Louisianians Can Take It," *Bulletin of the American Iris Society*, no. 127, October 1942, pp. 31-33.

"Louisiana's Gift to Gardens," *Bulletin of Australian and New Zealand Iris Society*, November 1949.

"Louisiana's Gift to Gardens," *Plants and Gardens*, vol. 6, Winter 1950, pp. 239-241.

"Magic Water," *Holland's*, July 1932.

"Native American Bulbs," *Home Gardening for the South*, vol 5, no. 3, March 1945, pp. 44-45.

"Native Bulbs, Hymenocallis, and Crinum," *Home Gardening for the South*, vol. 4, no. 1, January 1944, p. 7.

"Native Iris Journal 1945," *Home Gardening for the South*, vol. 4, nos. 7 and 8, July-August 1945, pp. 126-129, 131, 145.

"Native Landscape and Wild Life," in Mabel Brasher's *Louisiana: A Study of the State*, New York: Johnson Publishing Company, 1929, pp. 306-326.

"New Irises of Louisiana," *American Home*, vo. 11, no. 6, May 1934, pp. 375-377, (Frontispiece in color).

"A New Race of Garden Irises," *American Iris Society Bulletin*, no. 122, July 1951, pp. 62-66.

"A New Voice from the Old South," (about Ada Jack Carver), *Holland's*, January 1927.

"Now You Can Have Iris Around the Year," *Home Gardening for the South*, vol. 10, April 1950, pp. 94-97.

"Oh, Those Catalogs! It's Never Too Hot to Plan," *Home Gardening for the South*, vol. 6, no. 7, July 1946, p. 400.

"Old-Fashioned Shrubs," *Home Gardening for the South*, vol. 9, no. 2, February 1951, pp. 44-45, 52.

"Onward with Louisiana Irises," *American Iris Society Bulletin*, no. 113, April 1949, pp. 61-62.

"Over the Back Gate," *Holland's*, January 1932.

"Plant Asters for Fall," *Home Gardening for the South*, vol. 9, no. 4, April 1949, pp. 81, 96.

"Plenty to See," *American Iris Society Bulletin*, no. 121, April 1951, pp. 5-8.

"The Return of the Native Phlox," *Home Gardening for the South*, vol. 4, no. 6, June 1944, p. 104.

"The Romance of Ti Rouge," *Farm Life*, October 1927.

"Save, Oh Save!" *Home Gardening for the South*, Winter 1940-1941.

"Shade Does It," *Home Gardening for the South*, vol. 10, no. 6, June 1950, p. 143.

"Some Can Take It! Louisiana Irises Get Cold Test," *American Iris Society Bulletin*, no. 113, April 1949, pp. 67-69.

"Southern Songsters," *Holland's*, May 1932.

"Species Notes—Louisiana Seedlings," *American Iris Society Bulletin*, no. 103, October 1946, pp. 74-75.

"The Story of Louisiana Iris," *Home Gardening for the South*, vol. 4, no. 5, May 1944, pp. 84-85, 87.

"Successful Gardens," *Holland's*, vol. 53, no. 7, July 1934, pp. 26, 41.

"Three Beautiful Texas Shrubs," *Home Gardening for the South*, vol. 9, no. 3, March 1945, pp. 54-55.

"Trees and Wild Flowers of Natchitoches Parish," in Germaine Portre-Bobinski's *Natchitoches: The Up-to-date Oldest Town in Louisiana*, New Orleans: Dameron-Pierson Co., Ltd., 1936, pp. 185-188.

"Trees for Shade and Beauty . . . Elms," *Home Gardening for the South*, vol. 7, no. 10, November 1947, pp. 224-225, 230.

"Trees for Shade and Beauty . . . Oaks," *Home Gardening for the South*, vol. 8, no. 10, November 1948, pp. 245, 257.

"Two Native Shrubs for Home Gardens," *Home Gardening for the South*, vol. 3, no. 8, May 1943, p. 127.

"Vines for the South," *Holland's*, January 1931.

"Water Lilies," *Holland's*, vol. 54, no. 8, August 1935, pp. 20, 22-23.